JEN STORM   RYAN HOWE   ALICE RL   NICKOLEJ VILLIGER

LITTLE MOONS

HIGHWATER PRESS

Content Warning: This book includes scenes that deal with the subject of Missing and Murdered Indigenous Women, Girls, and Two-Spirit People (MMIWG2S). If you require support in relation to MMIWG2S, please call the national independent toll-free support line at 1-844-413-6649. This line is available 7 days a week, 24 hours a day, free of charge. You can find more information and aftercare services at www.mmiwg-ffada.ca/aftercare-services/. If you are in crisis in Canada or the United States, please call or text the Suicide Crisis Helpline at 988.

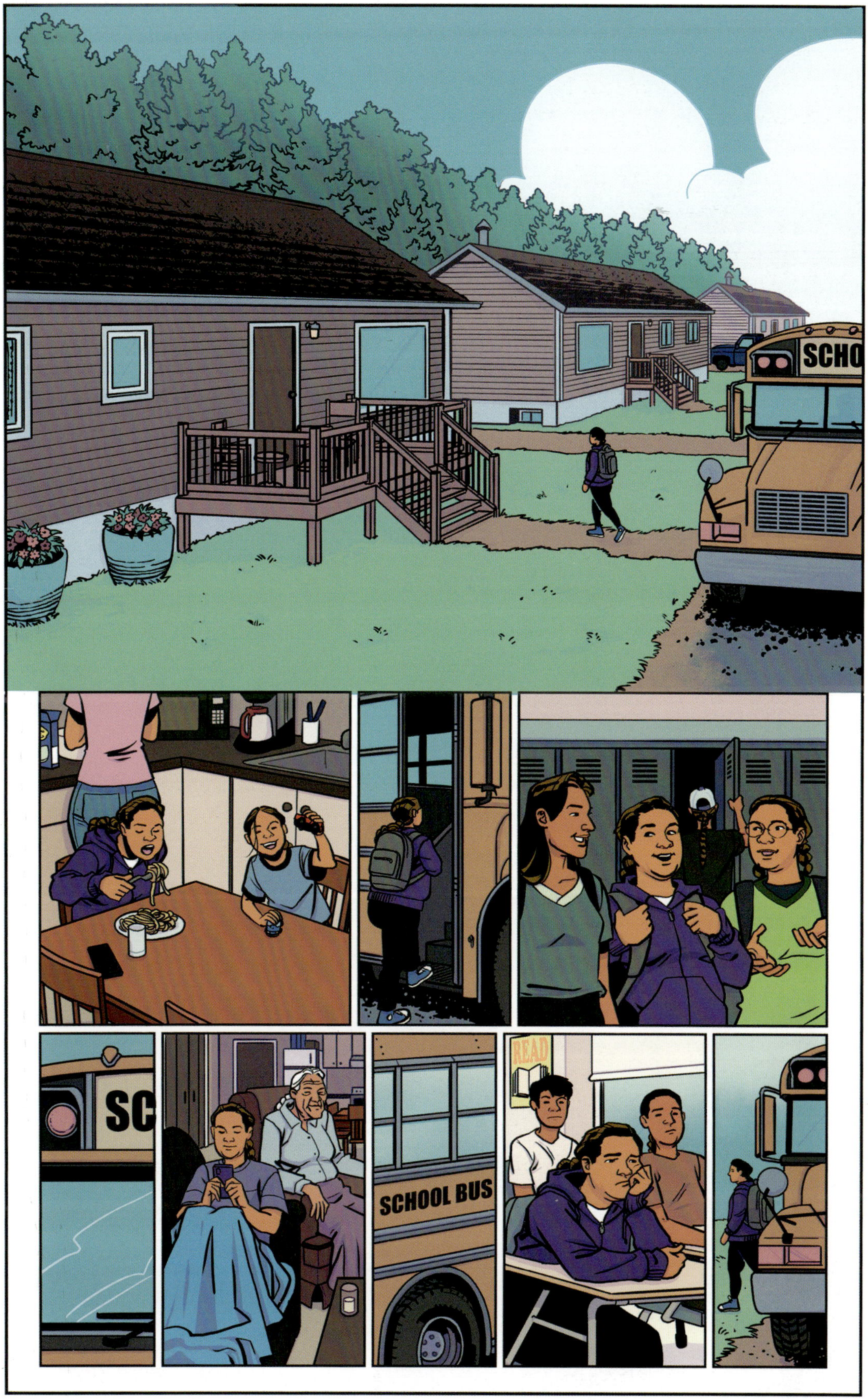
SCHO
SC
SCHOOL BUS
READ

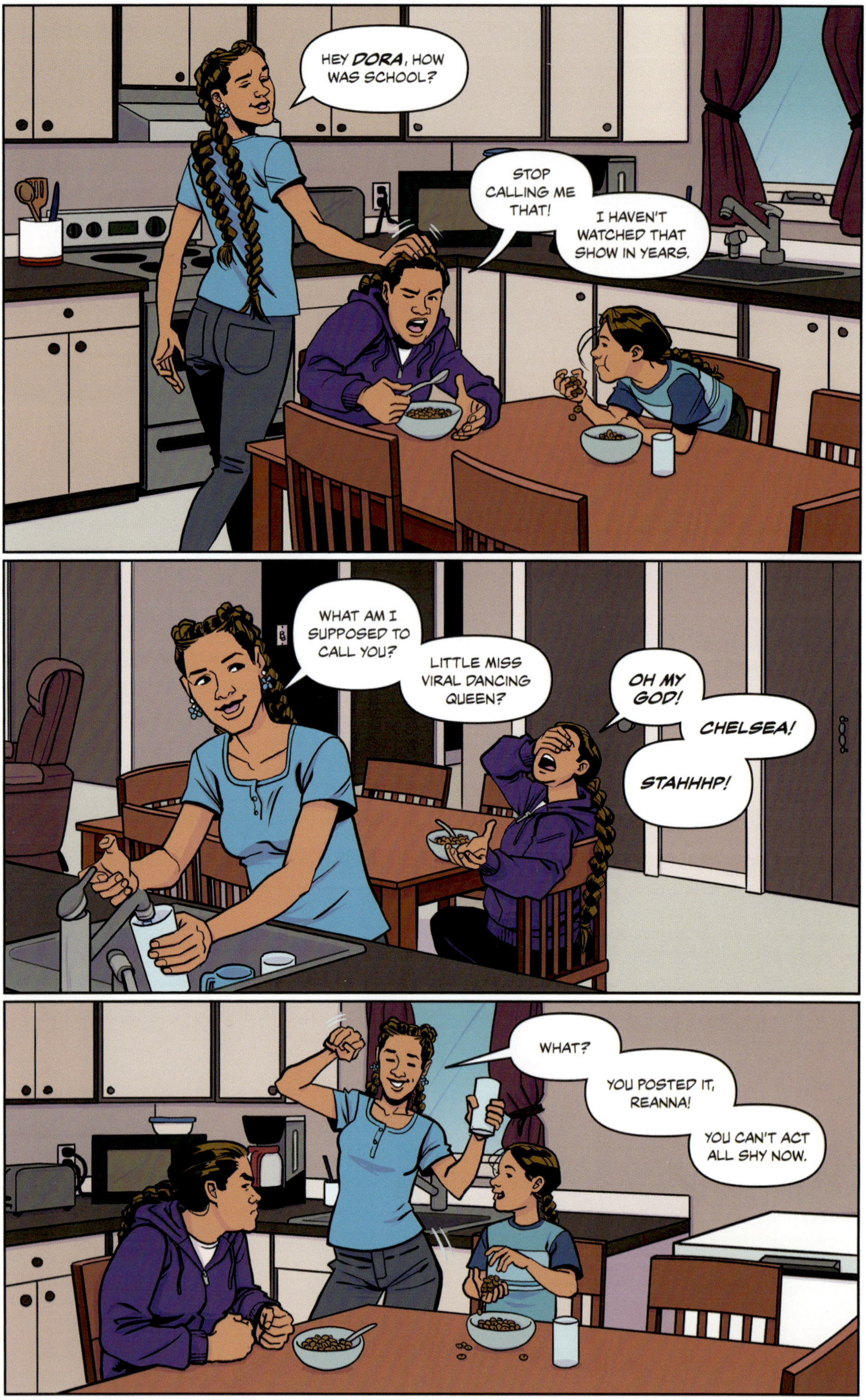
HEY *DORA*, HOW WAS SCHOOL?
STOP CALLING ME THAT!
I HAVEN'T WATCHED THAT SHOW IN YEARS.
WHAT AM I SUPPOSED TO CALL YOU?
LITTLE MISS VIRAL DANCING QUEEN?
OH MY GOD!
CHELSEA!
STAHHHP!
WHAT?
YOU POSTED IT, REANNA!
YOU CAN'T ACT ALL SHY NOW.

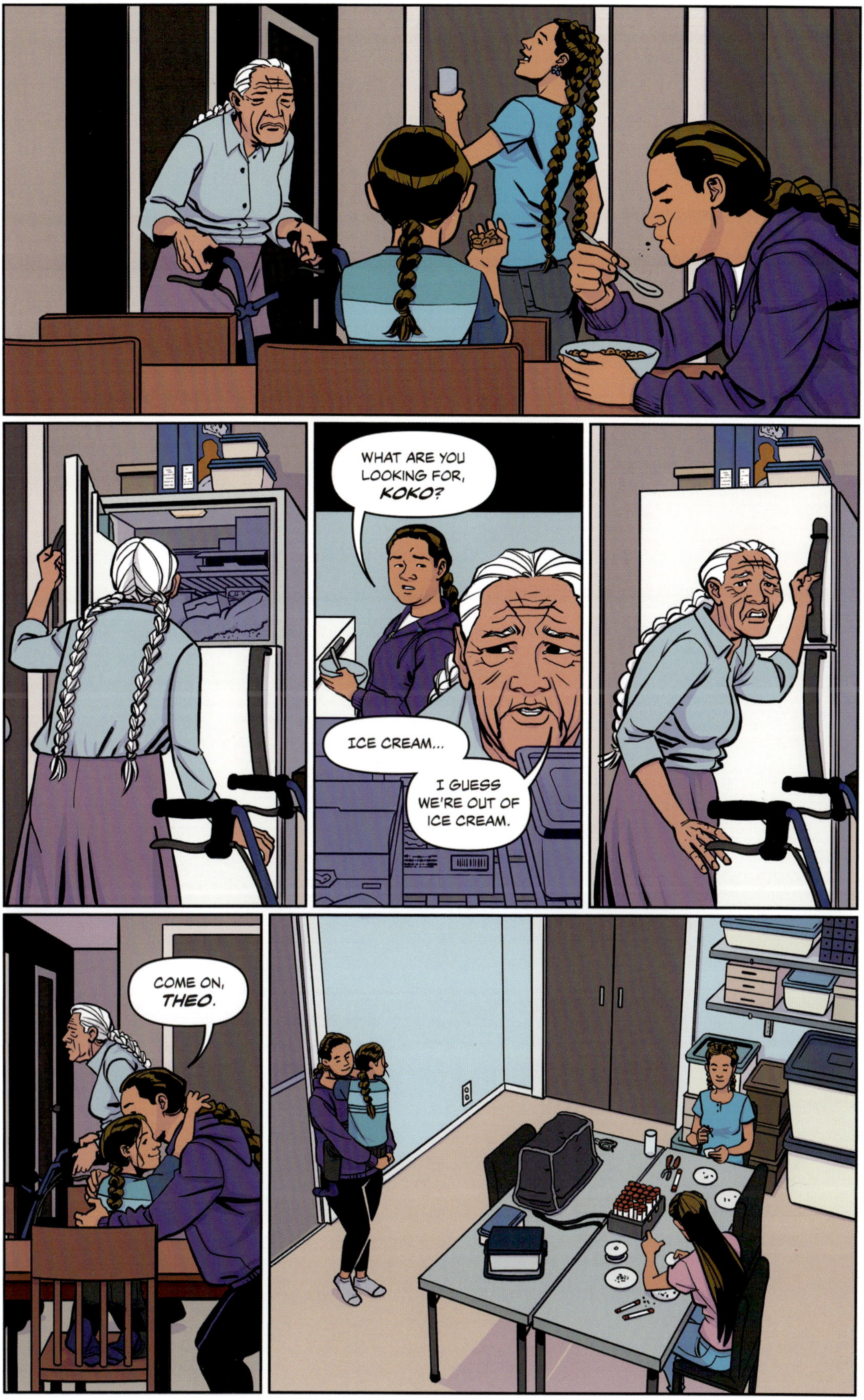

WHAT ARE YOU LOOKING FOR, KOKO?
ICE CREAM...
I GUESS WE'RE OUT OF ICE CREAM.
COME ON, THEO.

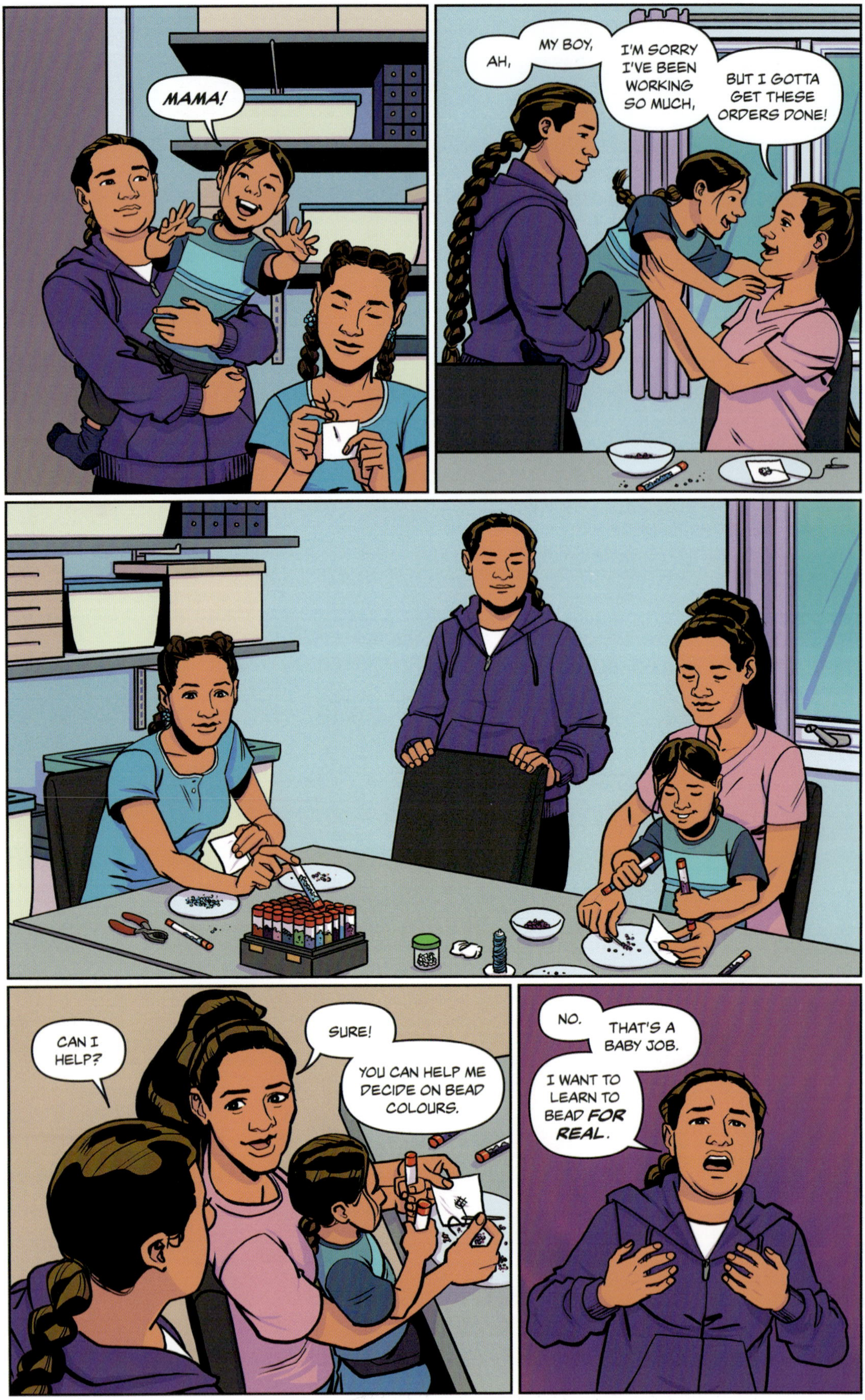
MAMA!
AH,
MY BOY,
I'M SORRY I'VE BEEN WORKING SO MUCH,
BUT I GOTTA GET THESE ORDERS DONE!
CAN I HELP?
SURE!
YOU CAN HELP ME DECIDE ON BEAD COLOURS.
NO.
THAT'S A BABY JOB.
I WANT TO LEARN TO BEAD **FOR REAL**.

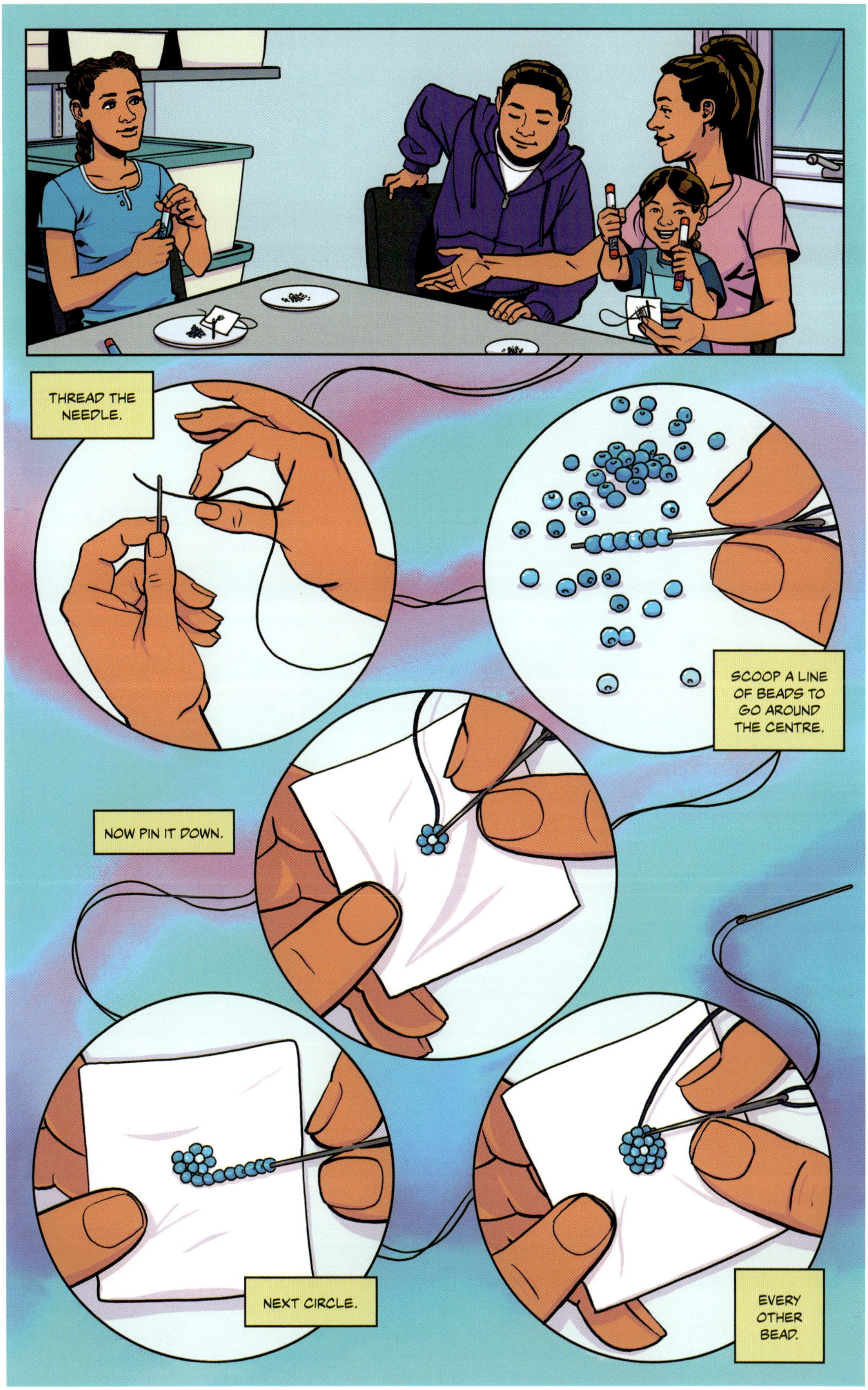
THREAD THE NEEDLE.
SCOOP A LINE OF BEADS TO GO AROUND THE CENTRE.
NOW PIN IT DOWN.
NEXT CIRCLE.
EVERY OTHER BEAD.

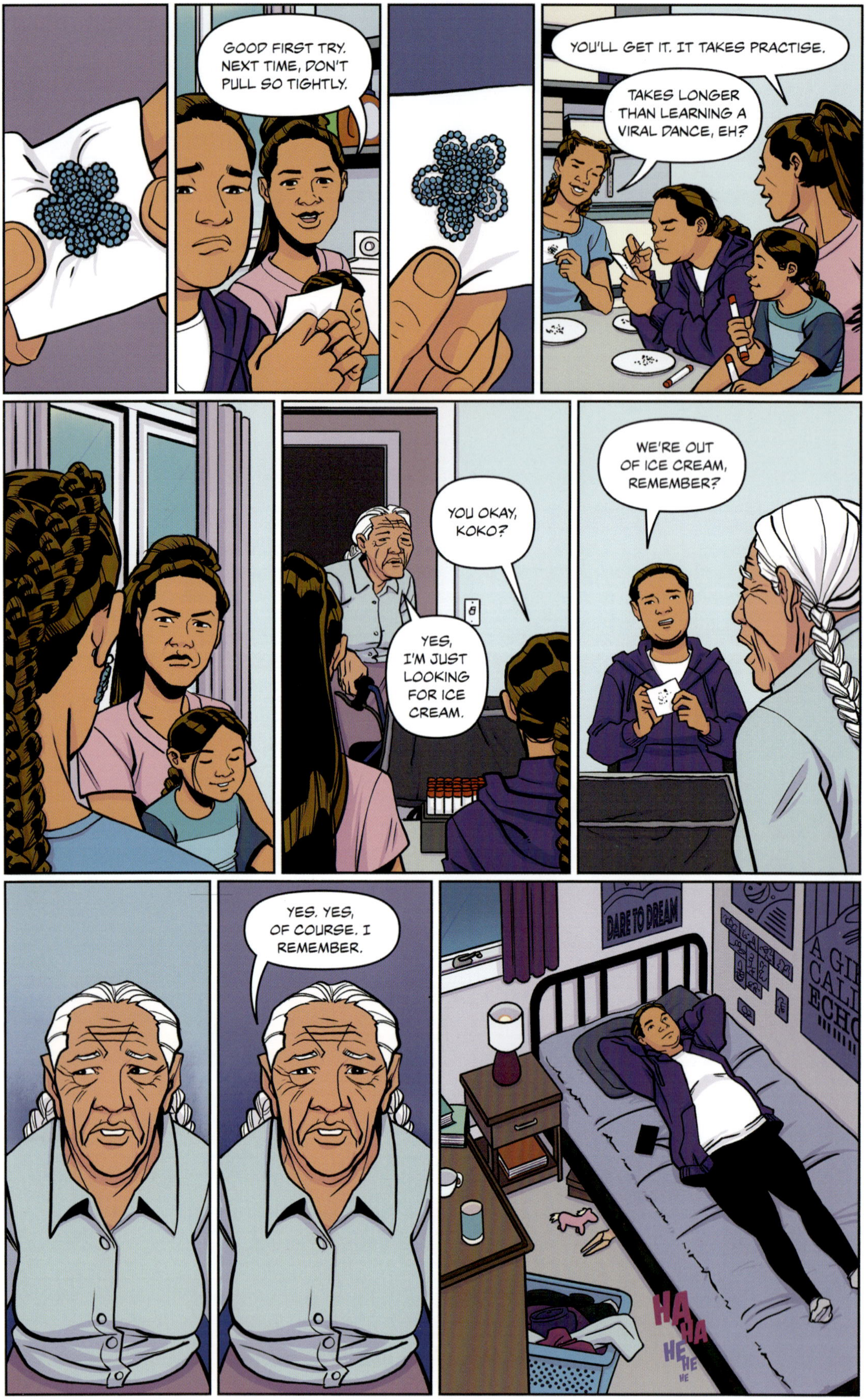
GOOD FIRST TRY. NEXT TIME, DON'T PULL SO TIGHTLY.
YOU'LL GET IT. IT TAKES PRACTISE.
TAKES LONGER THAN LEARNING A VIRAL DANCE, EH?
YOU OKAY, KOKO?
YES, I'M JUST LOOKING FOR ICE CREAM.
WE'RE OUT OF ICE CREAM, REMEMBER?
YES. YES, OF COURSE. I REMEMBER.
DARE TO DREAM
HA HA
HE HE HE

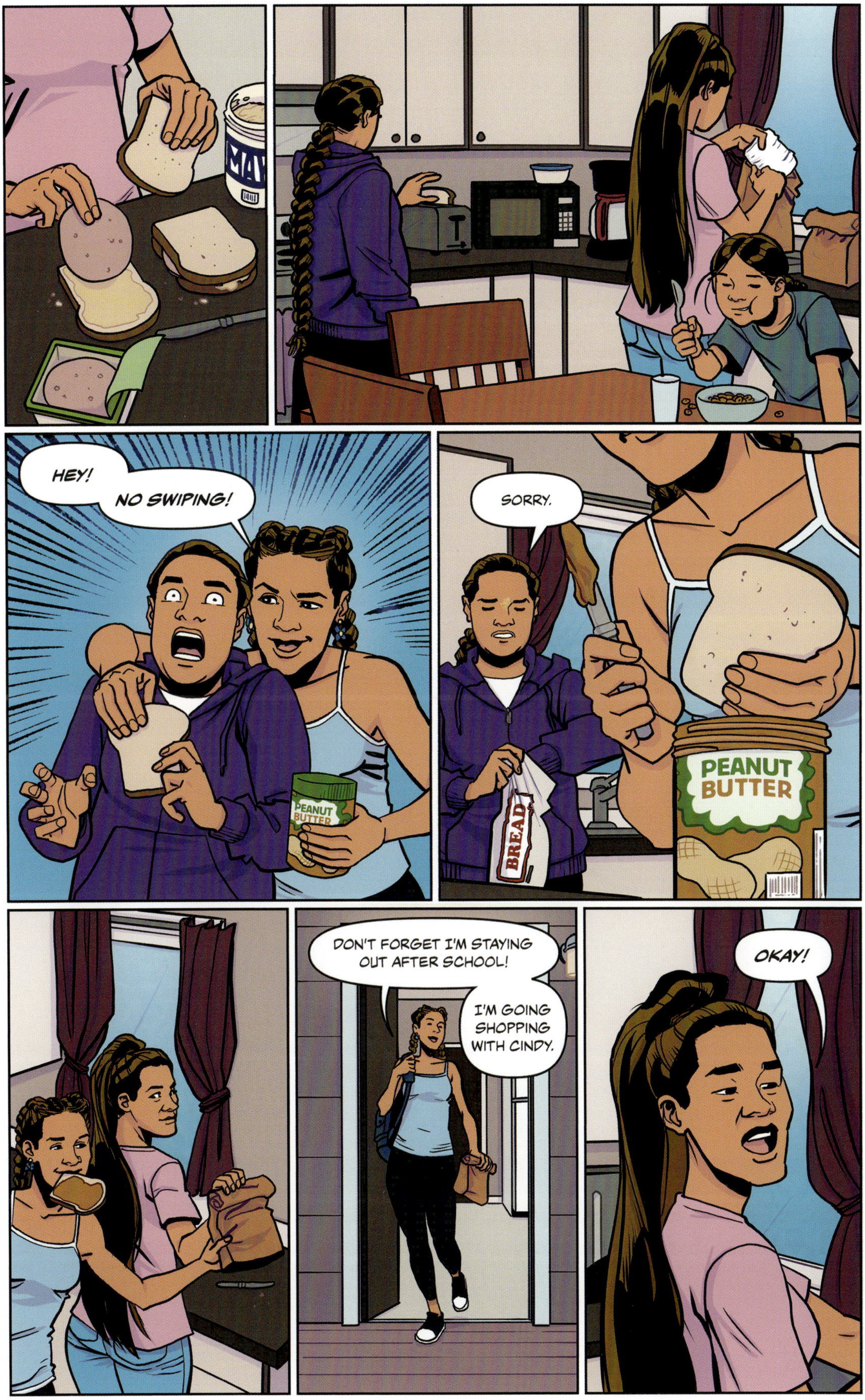
MAY
HEY!
NO SWIPING!
SORRY.
BREAD
PEANUT BUTTER
PEANUT BUTTER
DON'T FORGET I'M STAYING OUT AFTER SCHOOL!
I'M GOING SHOPPING WITH CINDY.
OKAY!

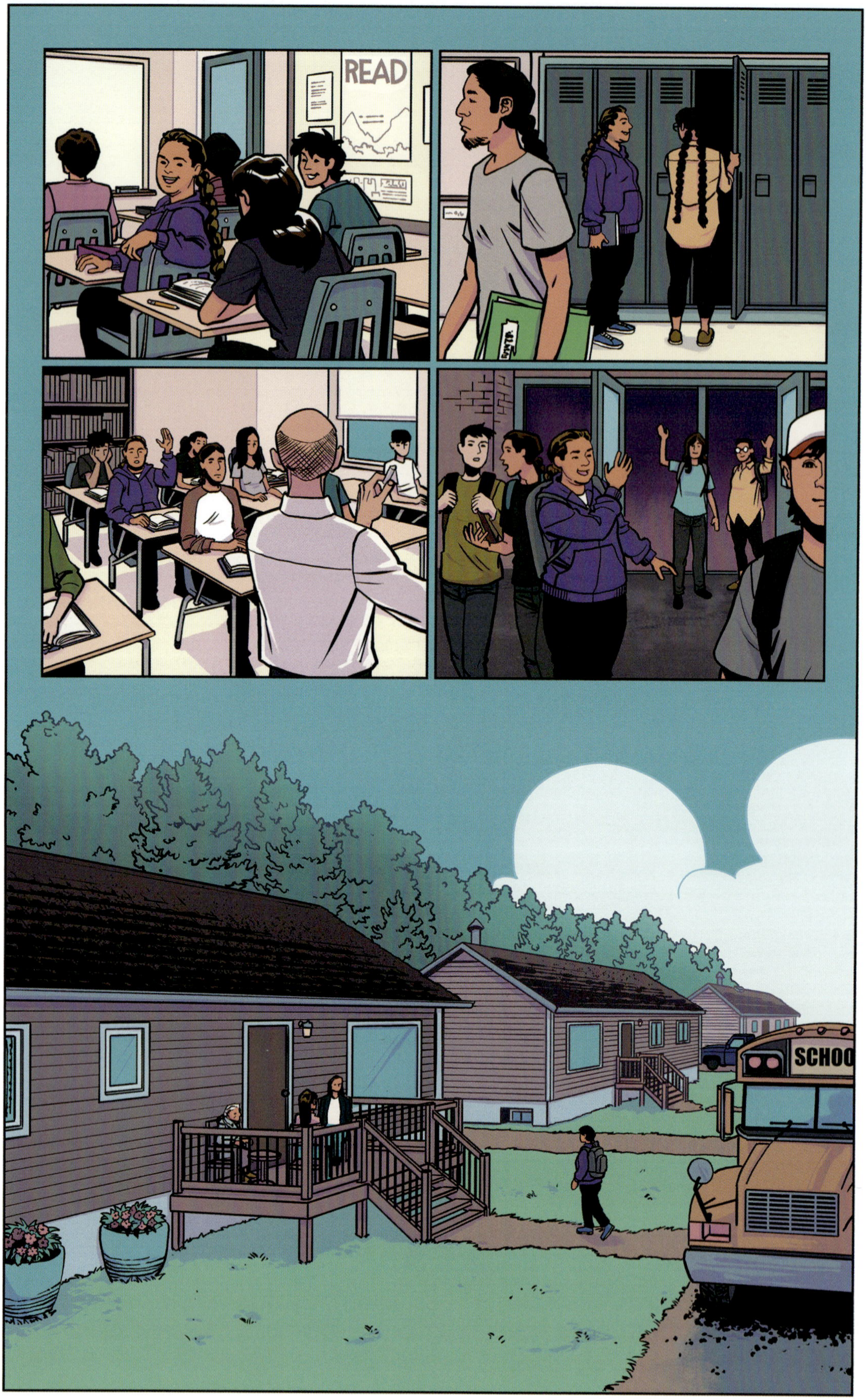
READ
SCHOO

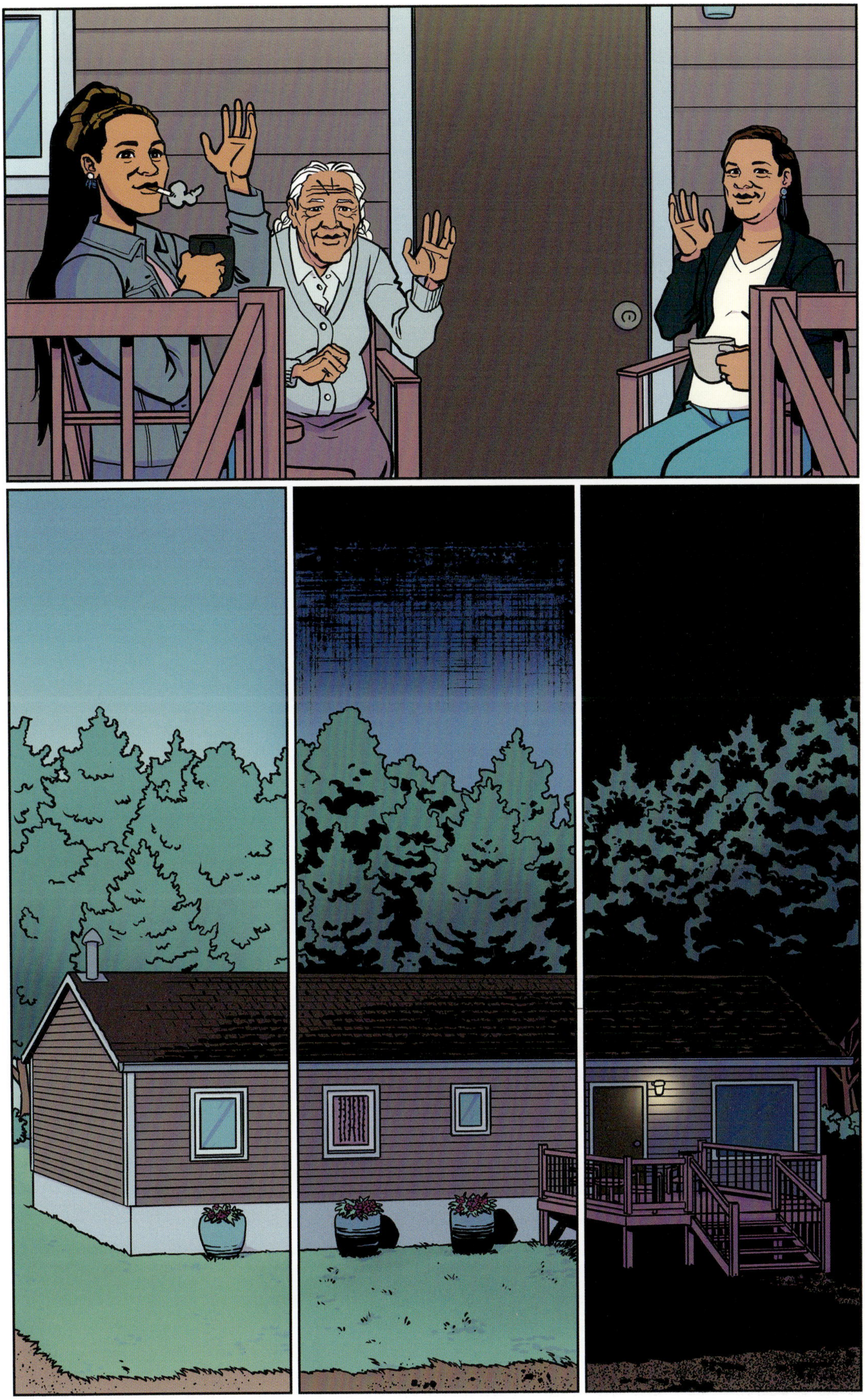

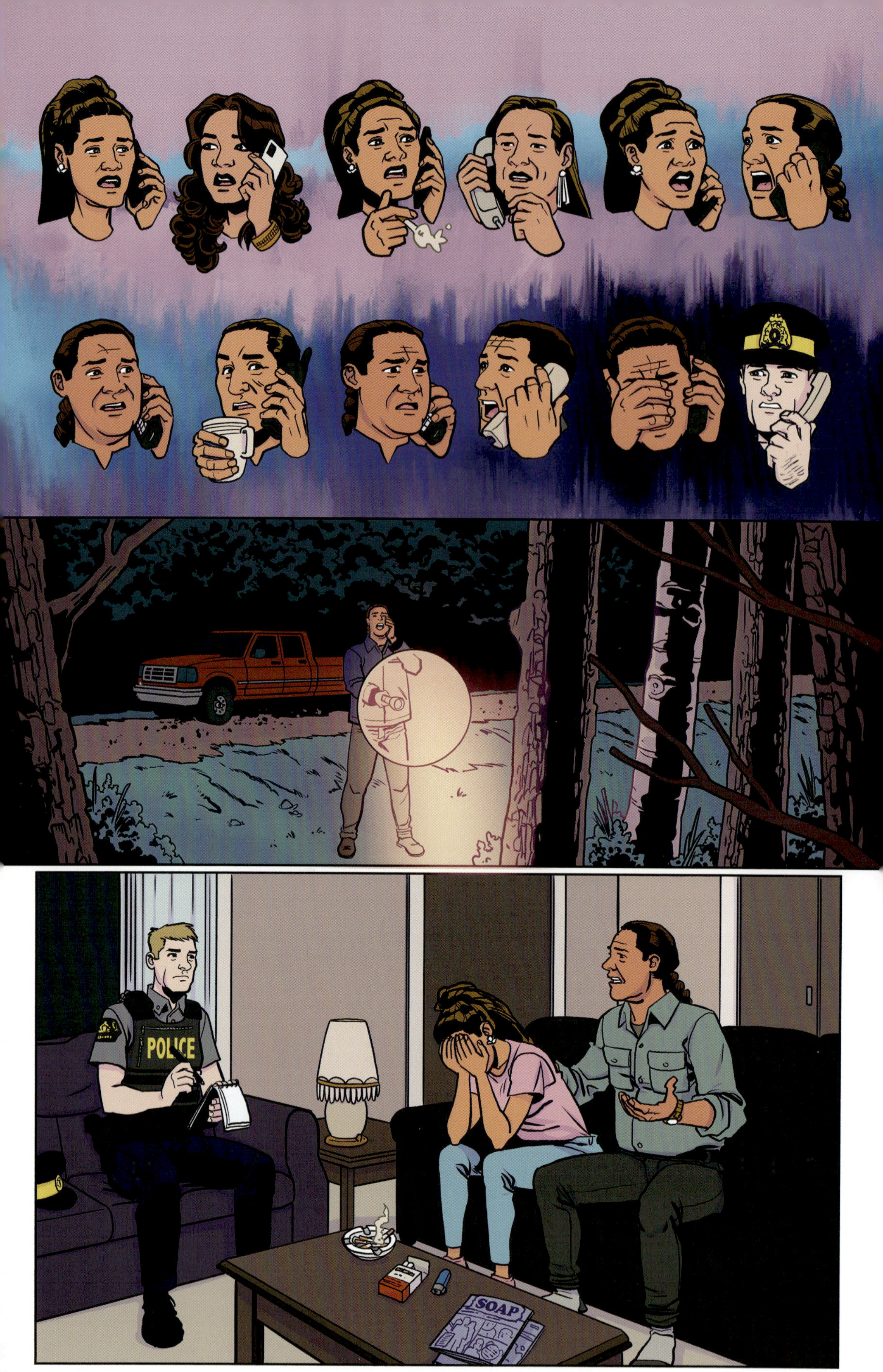
POLICE
SOAP

Plz Chelsea, let someone know you are alright, or connect with your mom!

Chelsea was last seen leaving school wearing a blue tank top and black jeans.

Anyone with information on Chelsea's whereabouts is asked to contact the RCMP.

The RCMP Missing Persons Unit is requesting assistance in locating a 15-year-old Indigenous female, 5'5" tall 115 lbs, with brown hair and eyes.

Plz if anybody has seen my niece Chelsea let my sister Andrea know! Her mom is very worried.

It's a parent's worst nightmare not knowing where their child is, thank you all for sharing the poster.

Chelsea is my young cousin. I hope and pray that someone sees this post and knows where she is.

If anyone knows Chelsea's whereabouts, please let us know. It's not like her to not contact us.

Has anyone seen Chelsea? She left school by herself saying she was only going to be gone a few hours.

Please contact us day or night if you hear anything from Chelsea and let us know she's safe!

Anyone heard from Chelsea? It's out of character for her to be away this long.

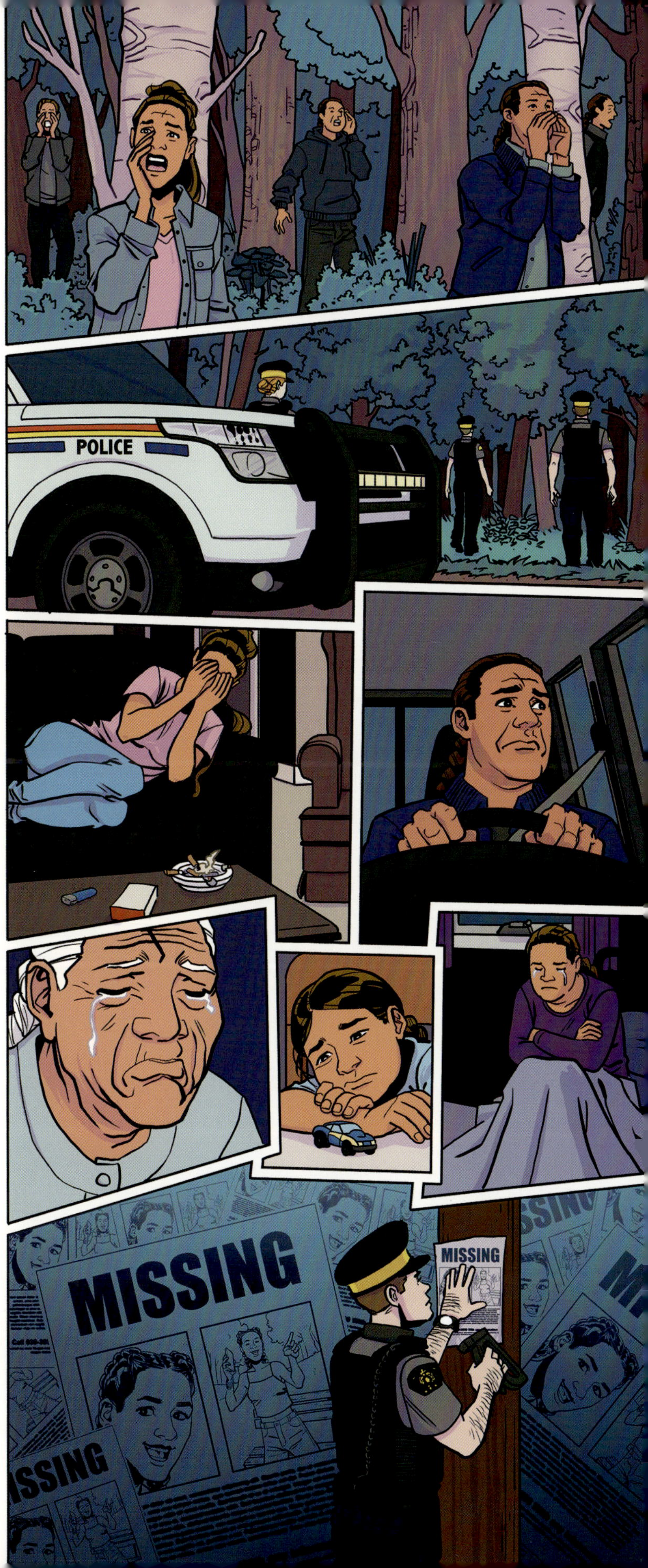
POLICE
MISSING
MISSING

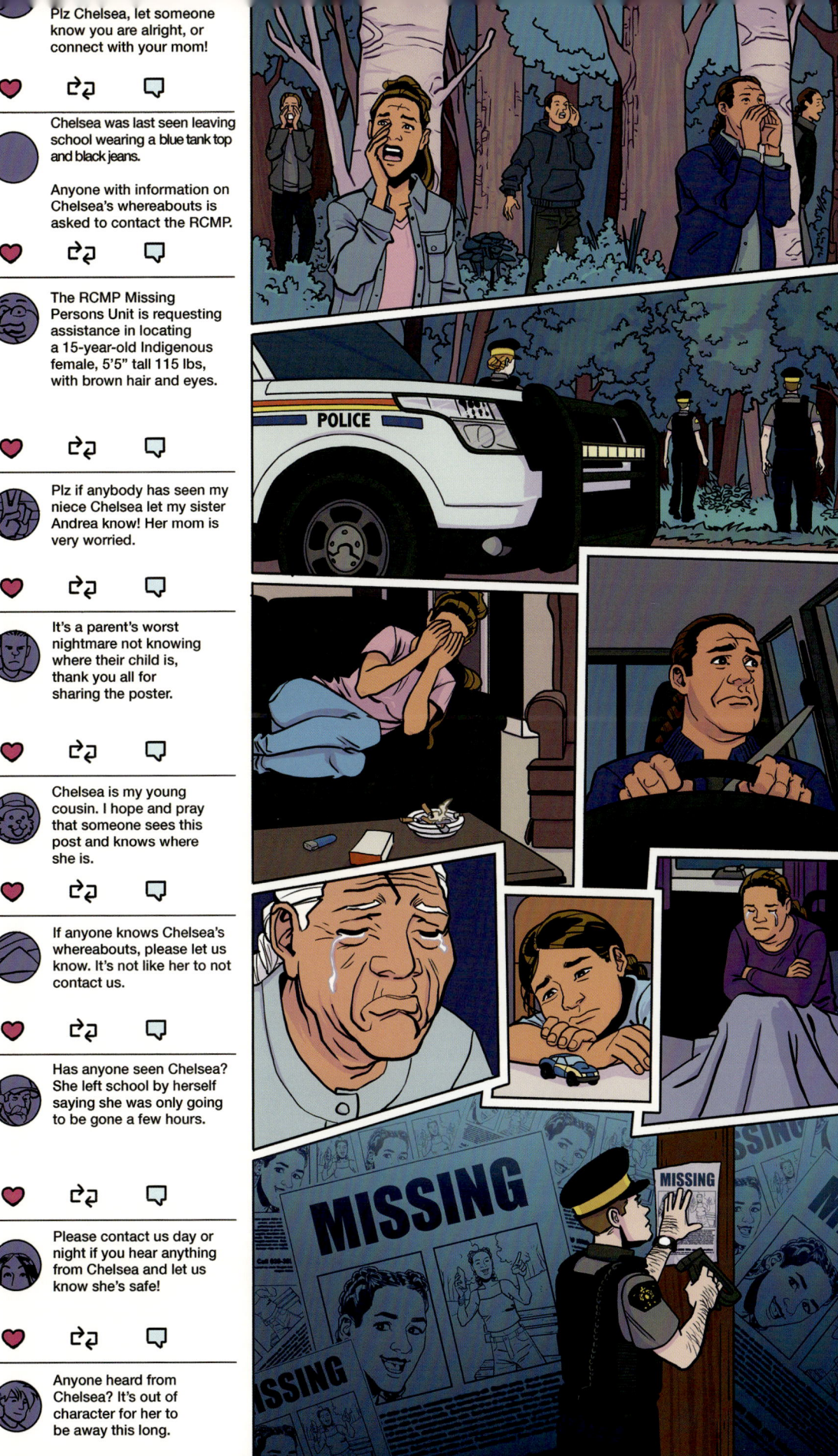

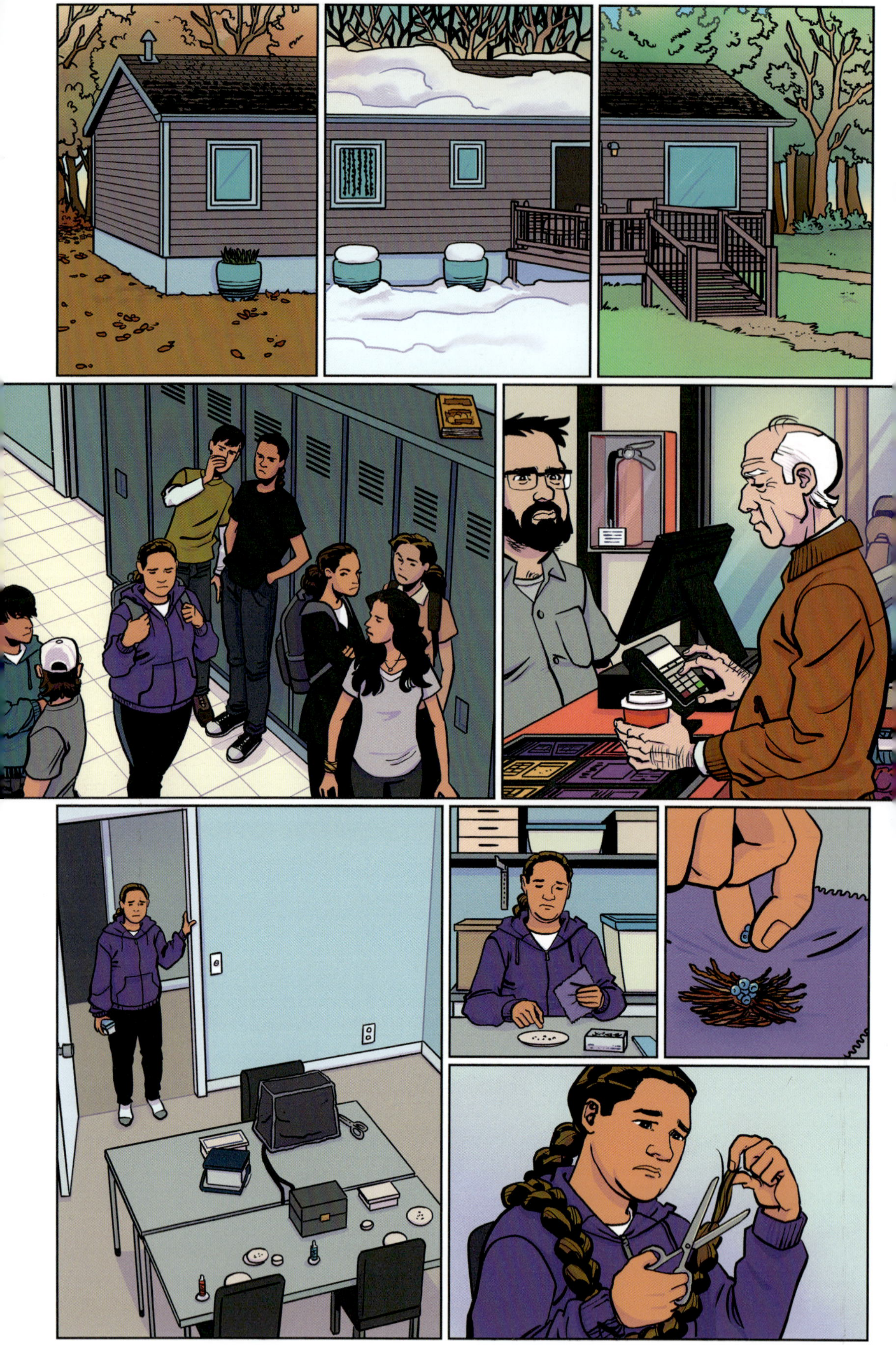

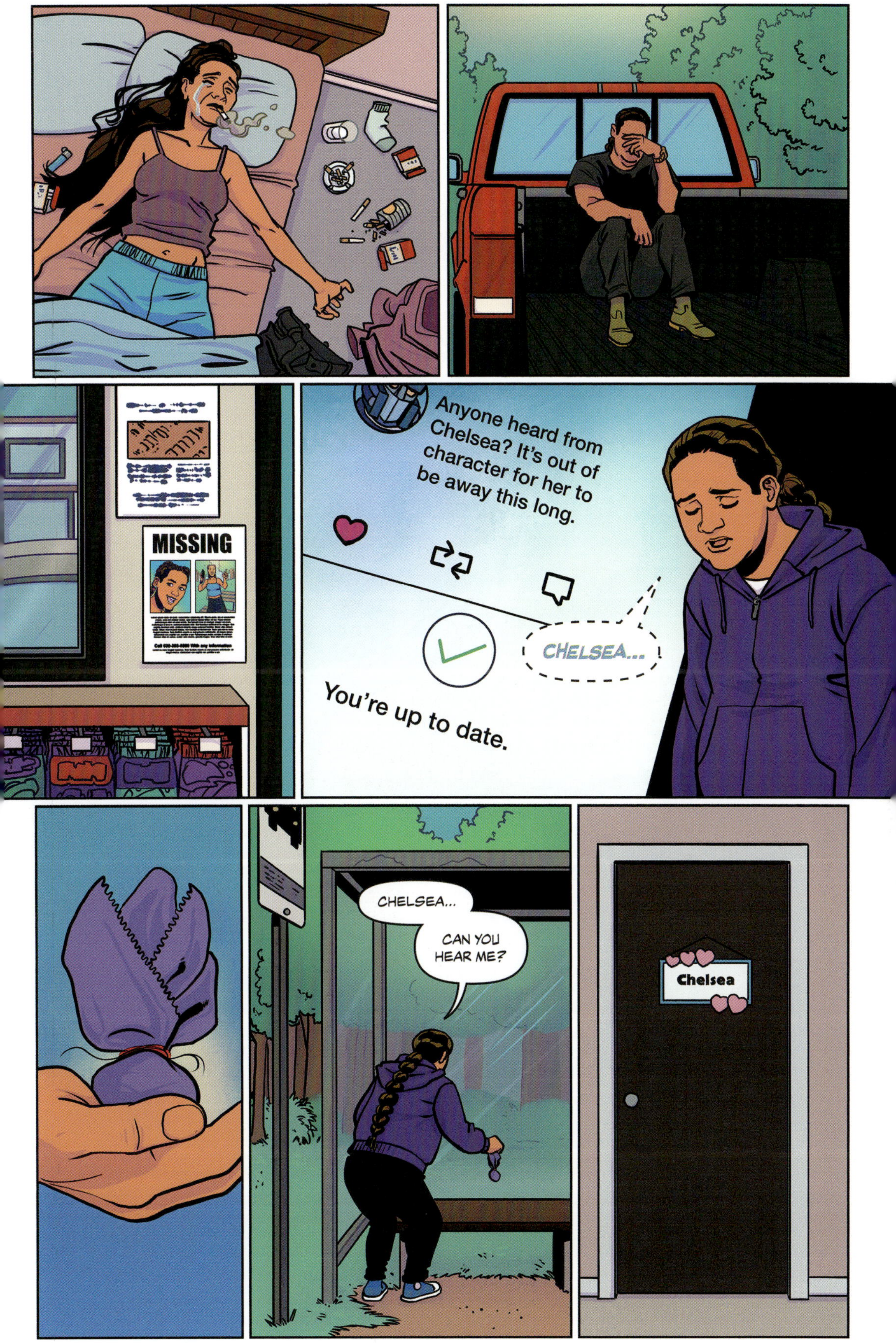
MISSING
Anyone heard from Chelsea? It's out of character for her to be away this long.
CHELSEA...
You're up to date.
CHELSEA...
CAN YOU HEAR ME?
Chelsea

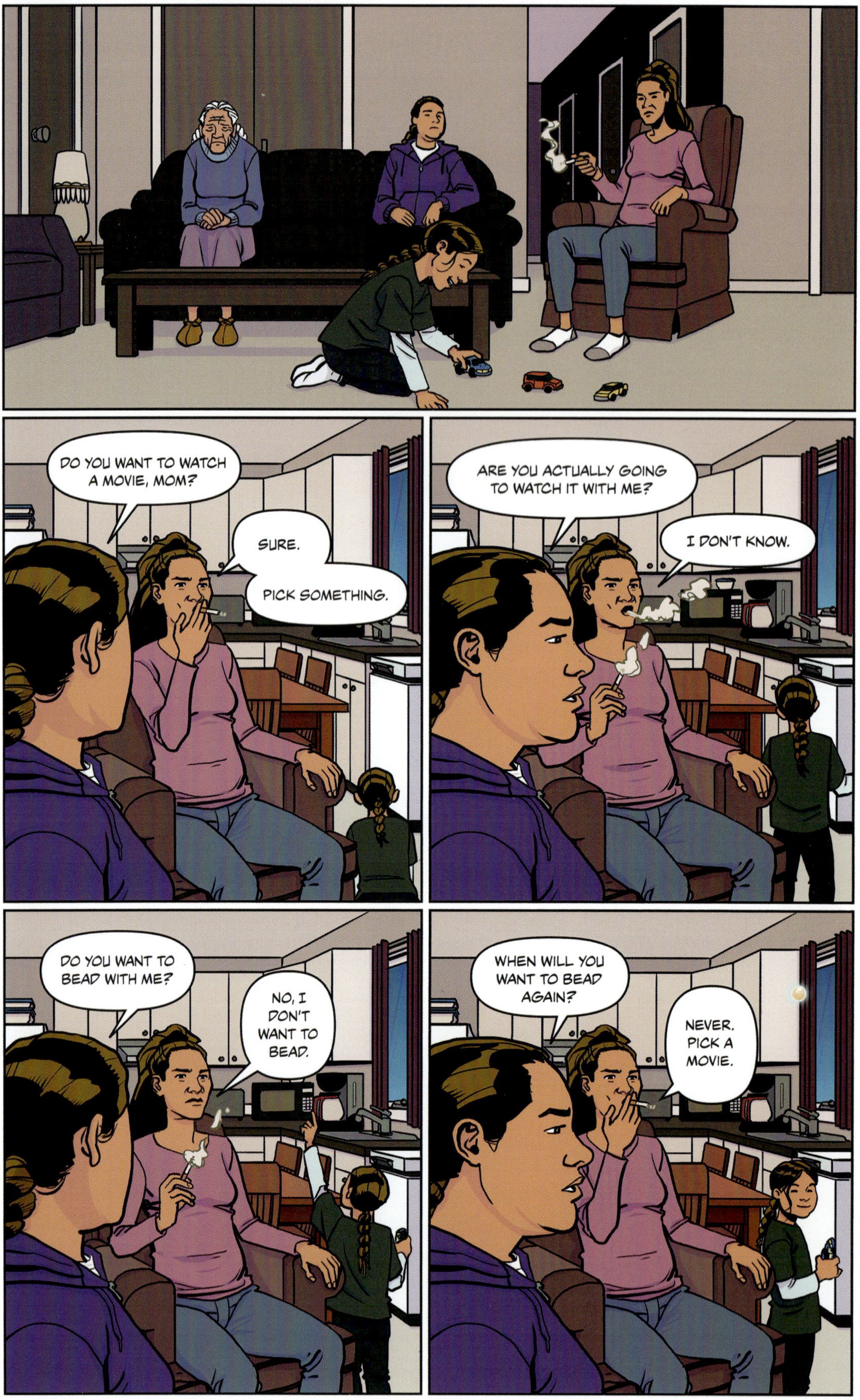
DO YOU WANT TO WATCH A MOVIE, MOM?
SURE.
PICK SOMETHING.
ARE YOU ACTUALLY GOING TO WATCH IT WITH ME?
I DON'T KNOW.
DO YOU WANT TO BEAD WITH ME?
NO, I DON'T WANT TO BEAD.
WHEN WILL YOU WANT TO BEAD AGAIN?
NEVER. PICK A MOVIE.

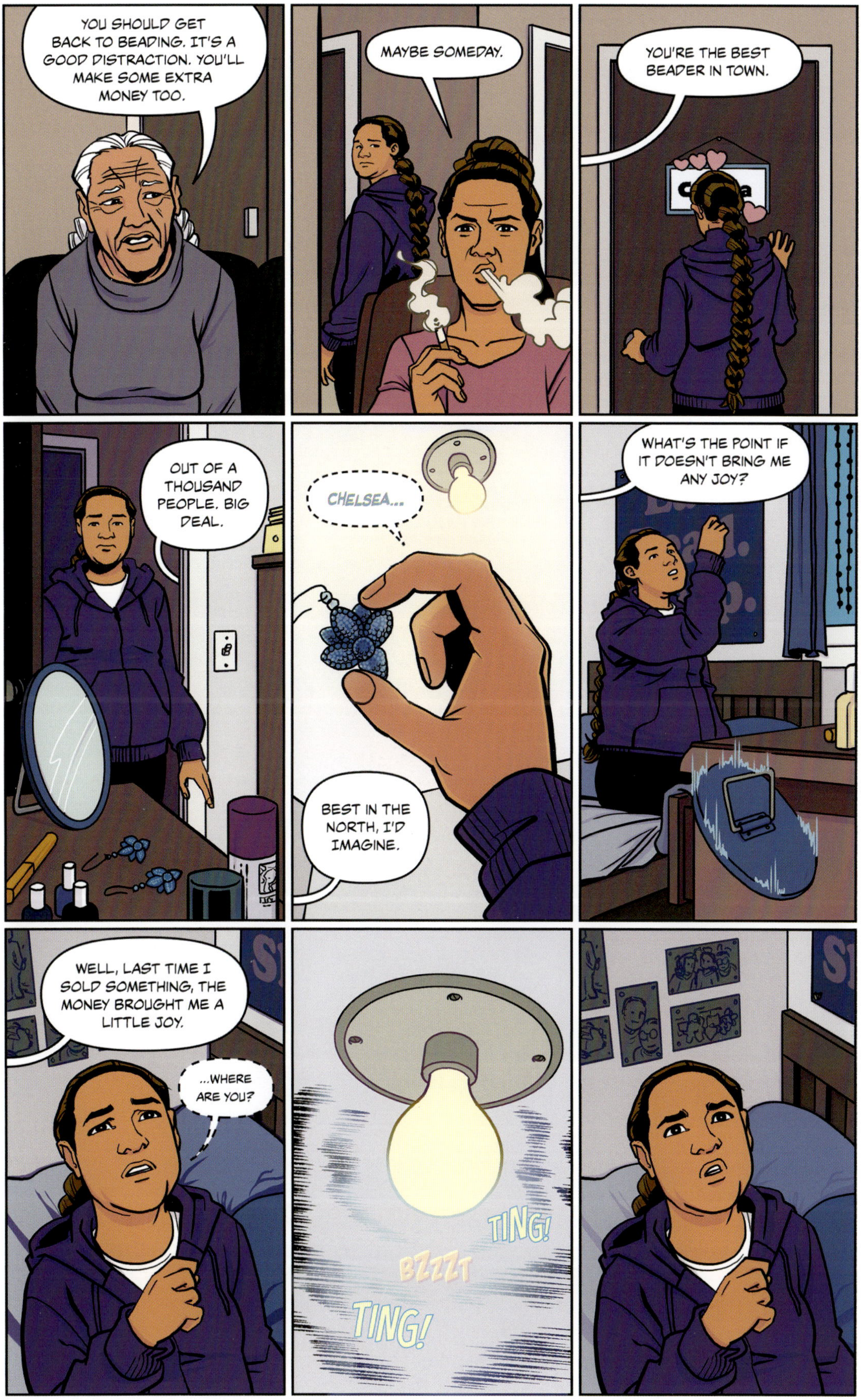
YOU SHOULD GET BACK TO BEADING. IT'S A GOOD DISTRACTION. YOU'LL MAKE SOME EXTRA MONEY TOO.
MAYBE SOMEDAY.
YOU'RE THE BEST BEADER IN TOWN.
OUT OF A THOUSAND PEOPLE. BIG DEAL.
CHELSEA...
BEST IN THE NORTH, I'D IMAGINE.
WHAT'S THE POINT IF IT DOESN'T BRING ME ANY JOY?
WELL, LAST TIME I SOLD SOMETHING, THE MONEY BROUGHT ME A LITTLE JOY.
...WHERE ARE YOU?
TING!
BZZZT
TING!

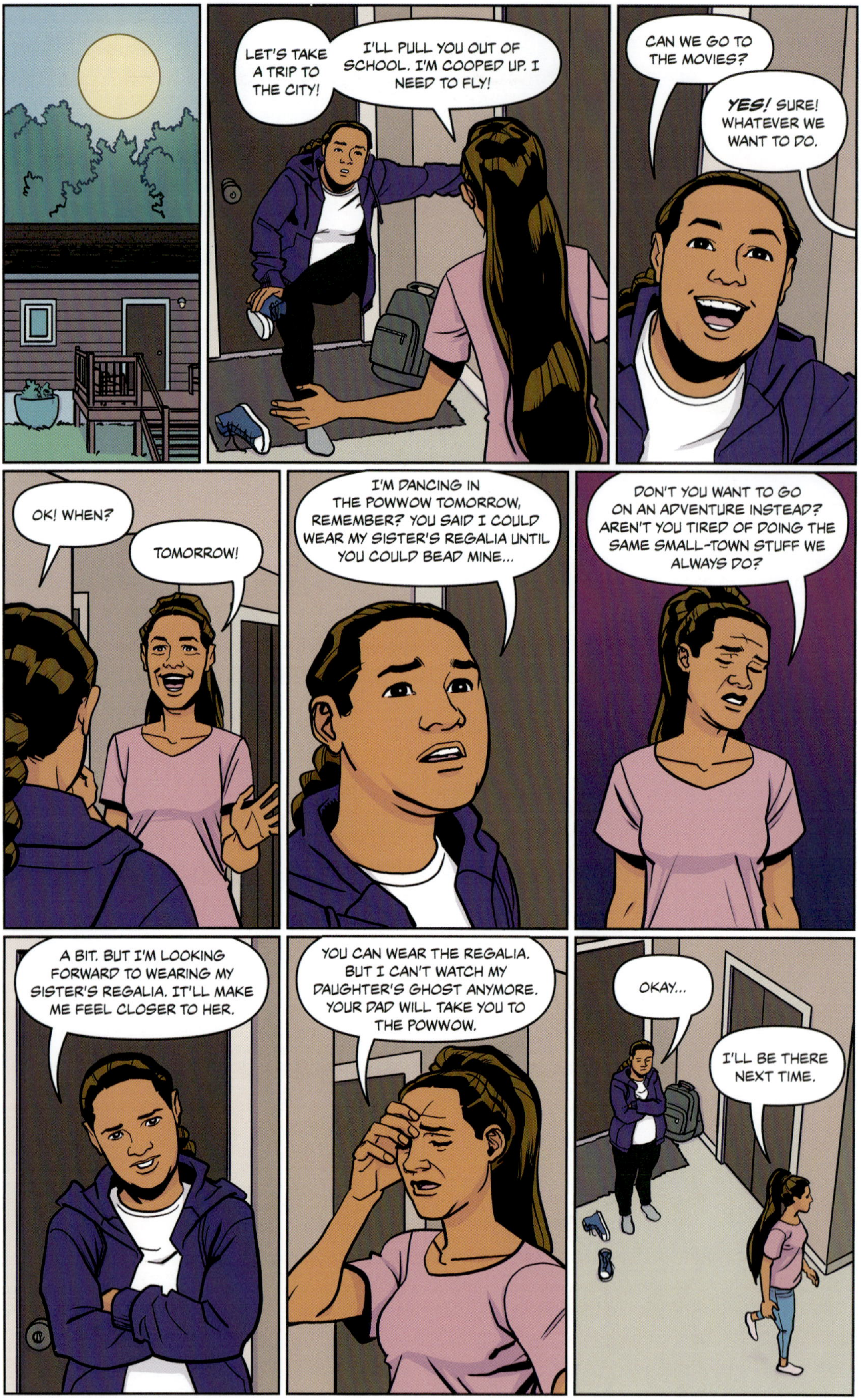
LET'S TAKE A TRIP TO THE CITY!
I'LL PULL YOU OUT OF SCHOOL. I'M COOPED UP. I NEED TO FLY!
CAN WE GO TO THE MOVIES?
YES! SURE! WHATEVER WE WANT TO DO.
OK! WHEN?
TOMORROW!
I'M DANCING IN THE POWWOW TOMORROW, REMEMBER? YOU SAID I COULD WEAR MY SISTER'S REGALIA UNTIL YOU COULD BEAD MINE...
DON'T YOU WANT TO GO ON AN ADVENTURE INSTEAD? AREN'T YOU TIRED OF DOING THE SAME SMALL-TOWN STUFF WE ALWAYS DO?
A BIT. BUT I'M LOOKING FORWARD TO WEARING MY SISTER'S REGALIA. IT'LL MAKE ME FEEL CLOSER TO HER.
YOU CAN WEAR THE REGALIA. BUT I CAN'T WATCH MY DAUGHTER'S GHOST ANYMORE. YOUR DAD WILL TAKE YOU TO THE POWWOW.
OKAY...
I'LL BE THERE NEXT TIME.

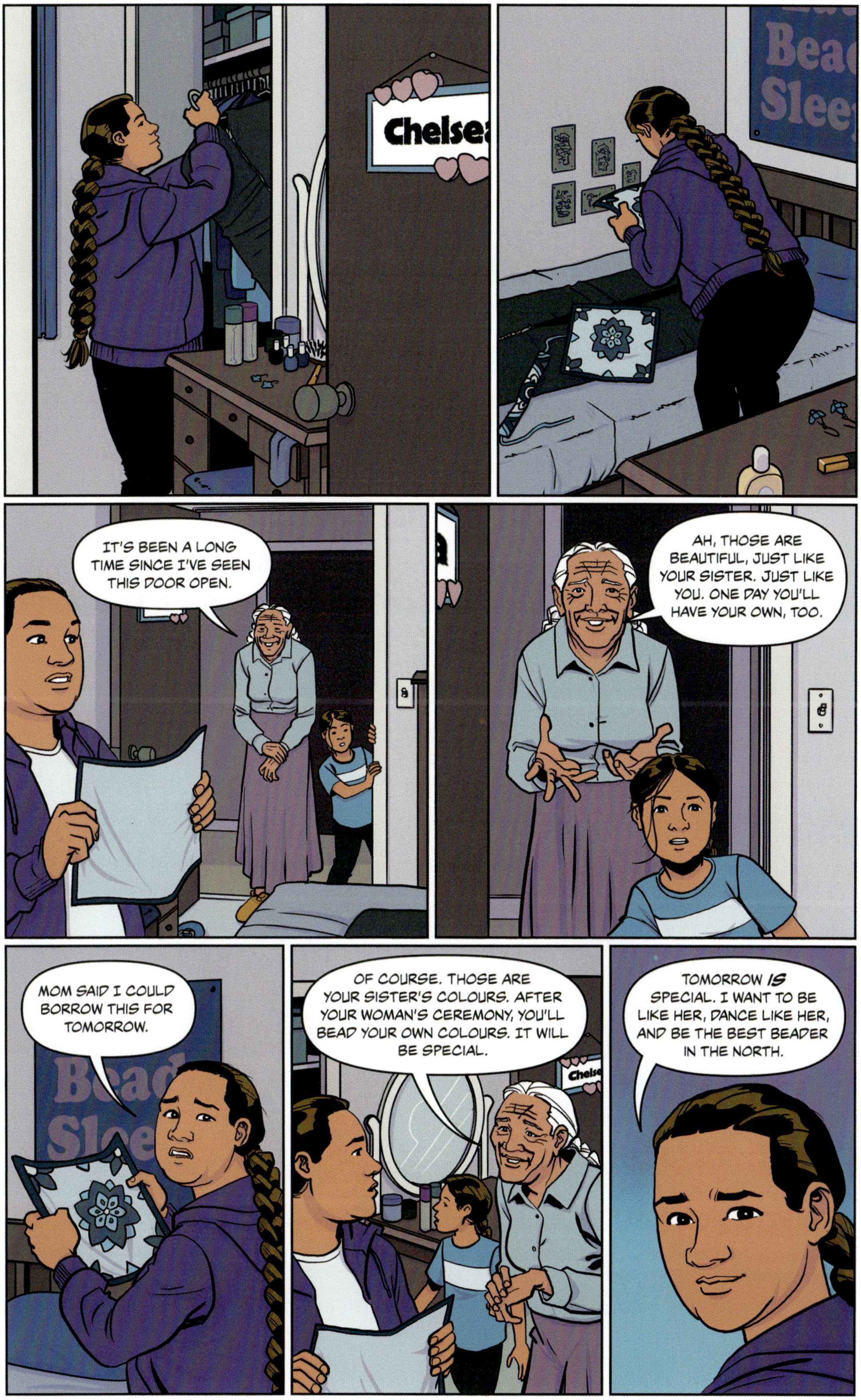
IT'S BEEN A LONG TIME SINCE I'VE SEEN THIS DOOR OPEN.
AH, THOSE ARE BEAUTIFUL, JUST LIKE YOUR SISTER. JUST LIKE YOU. ONE DAY YOU'LL HAVE YOUR OWN, TOO.
MOM SAID I COULD BORROW THIS FOR TOMORROW.
OF COURSE. THOSE ARE YOUR SISTER'S COLOURS. AFTER YOUR WOMAN'S CEREMONY, YOU'LL BEAD YOUR OWN COLOURS. IT WILL BE SPECIAL.
TOMORROW *IS* SPECIAL. I WANT TO BE LIKE HER, DANCE LIKE HER, AND BE THE BEST BEADER IN THE NORTH.

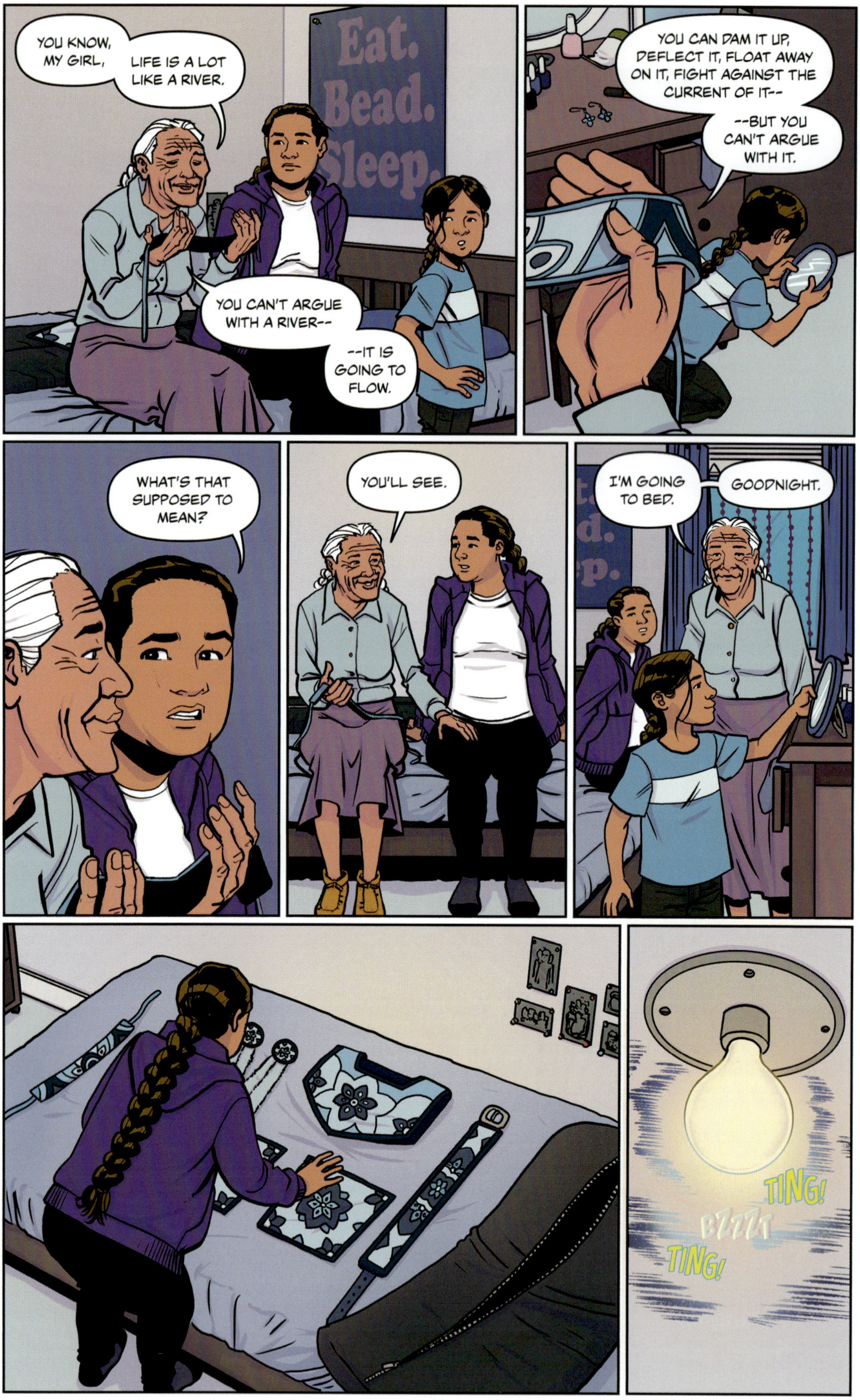
Eat. Bead. Sleep.
YOU KNOW, MY GIRL,
LIFE IS A LOT LIKE A RIVER.
YOU CAN'T ARGUE WITH A RIVER--
--IT IS GOING TO FLOW.
YOU CAN DAM IT UP, DEFLECT IT, FLOAT AWAY ON IT, FIGHT AGAINST THE CURRENT OF IT--
--BUT YOU CAN'T ARGUE WITH IT.
WHAT'S THAT SUPPOSED TO MEAN?
YOU'LL SEE.
I'M GOING TO BED.
GOODNIGHT.
TING!
BZZZT
TING!

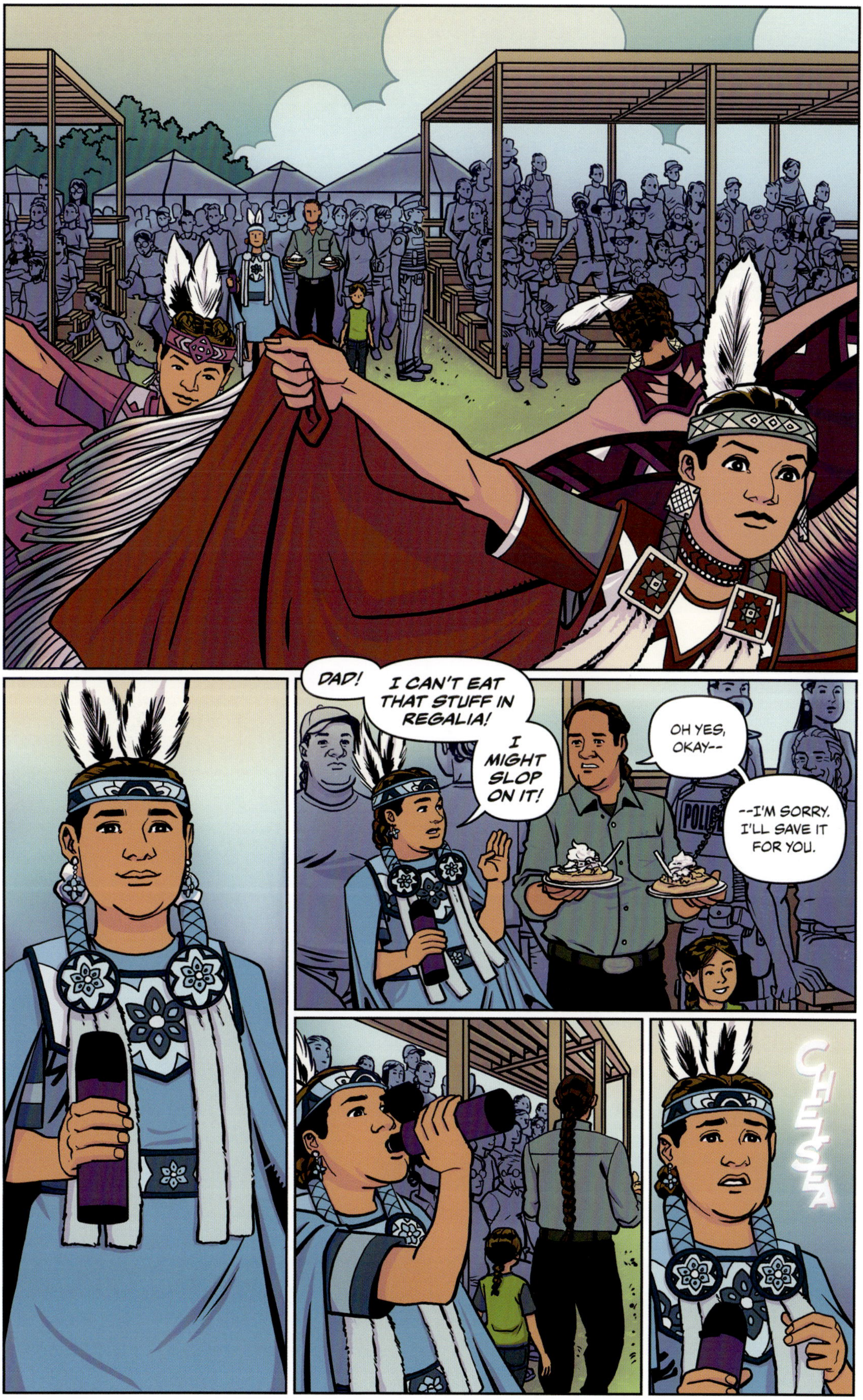
DAD!
I CAN'T EAT THAT STUFF IN REGALIA!
I MIGHT SLOP ON IT!
OH YES, OKAY--
--I'M SORRY. I'LL SAVE IT FOR YOU.
POLICE
CHELSEA

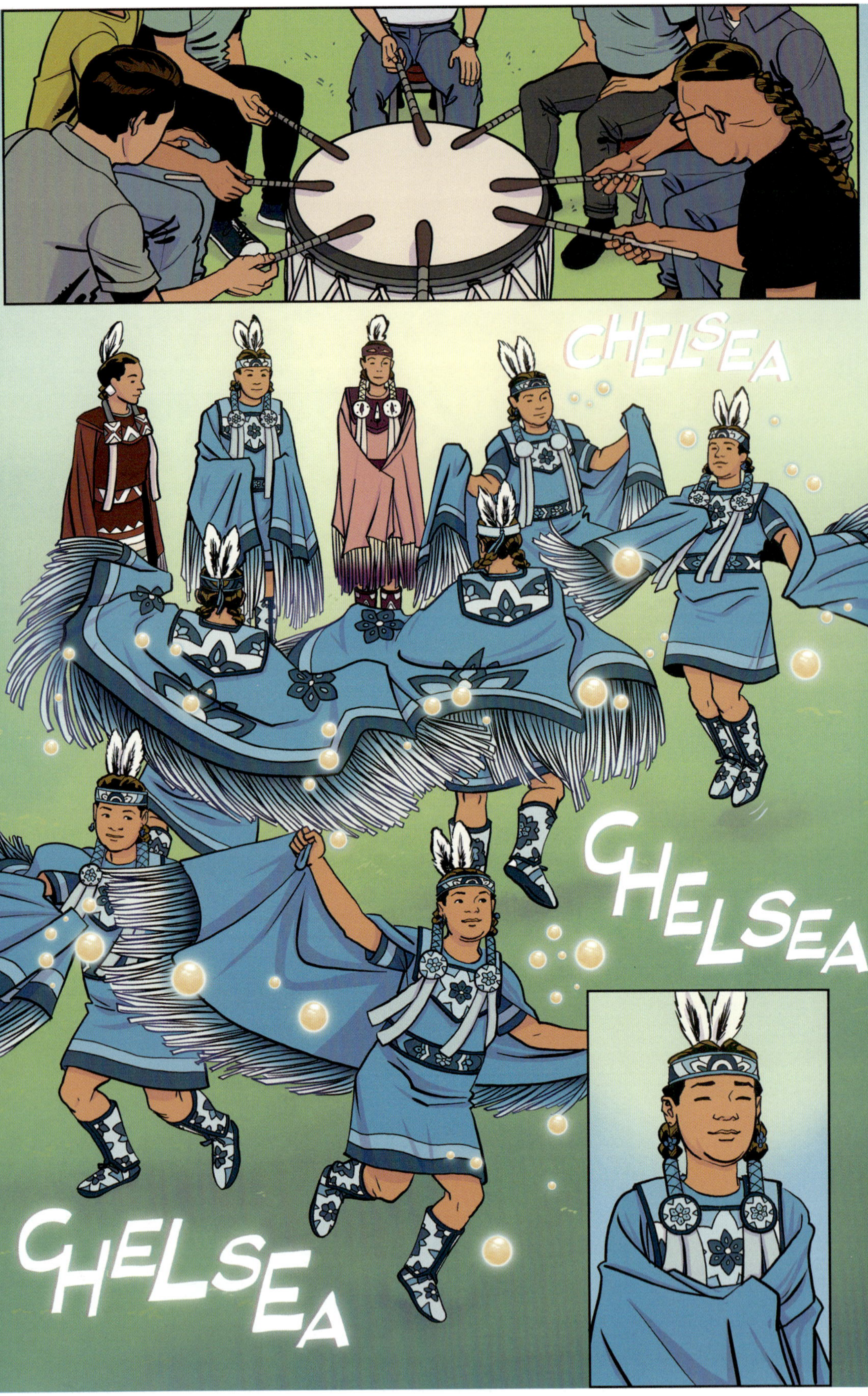
CHELSEA
CHELSEA
CHELSEA

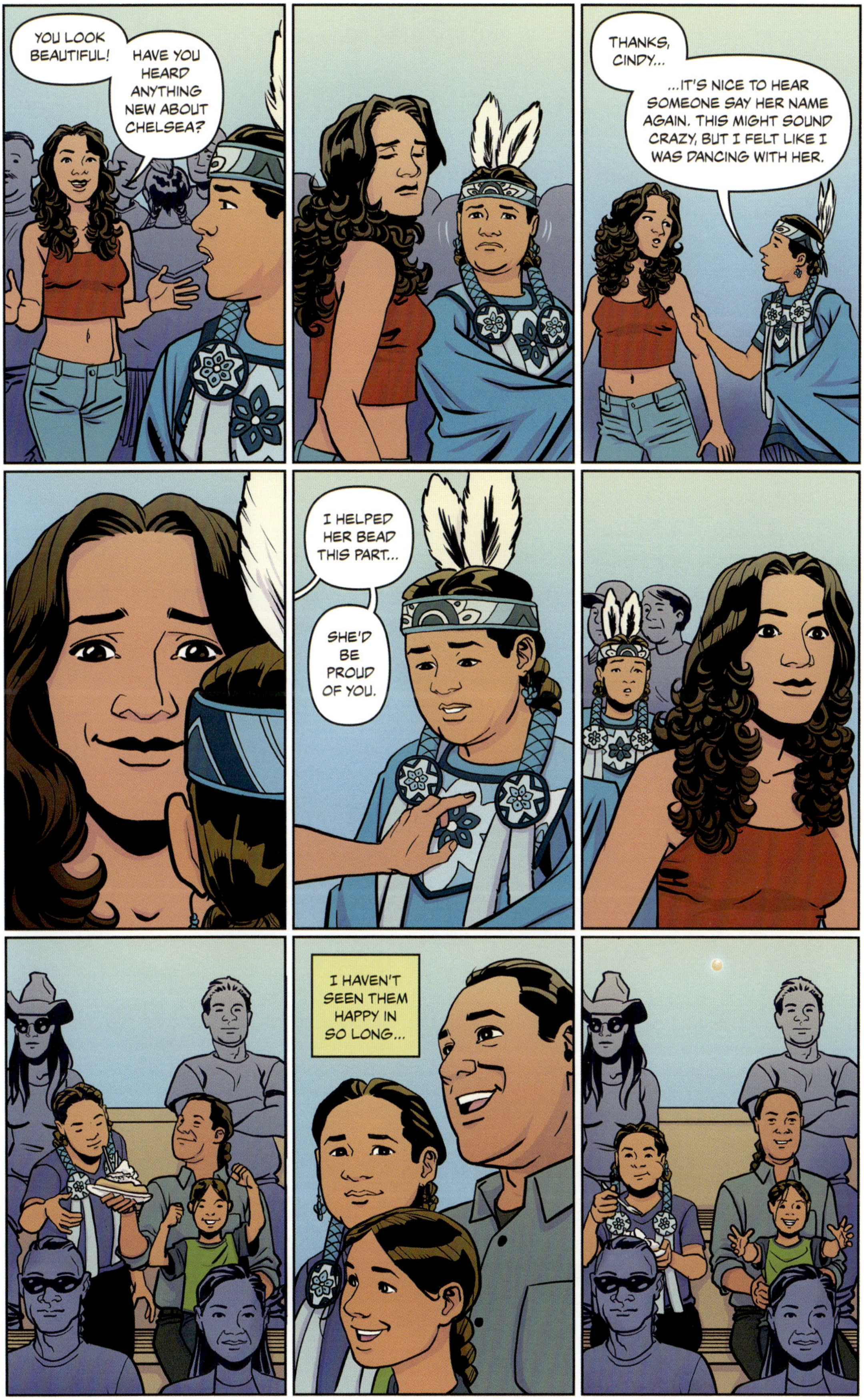
YOU LOOK BEAUTIFUL!
HAVE YOU HEARD ANYTHING NEW ABOUT CHELSEA?
THANKS, CINDY...
...IT'S NICE TO HEAR SOMEONE SAY HER NAME AGAIN. THIS MIGHT SOUND CRAZY, BUT I FELT LIKE I WAS DANCING WITH HER.
I HELPED HER BEAD THIS PART...
SHE'D BE PROUD OF YOU.
I HAVEN'T SEEN THEM HAPPY IN SO LONG...

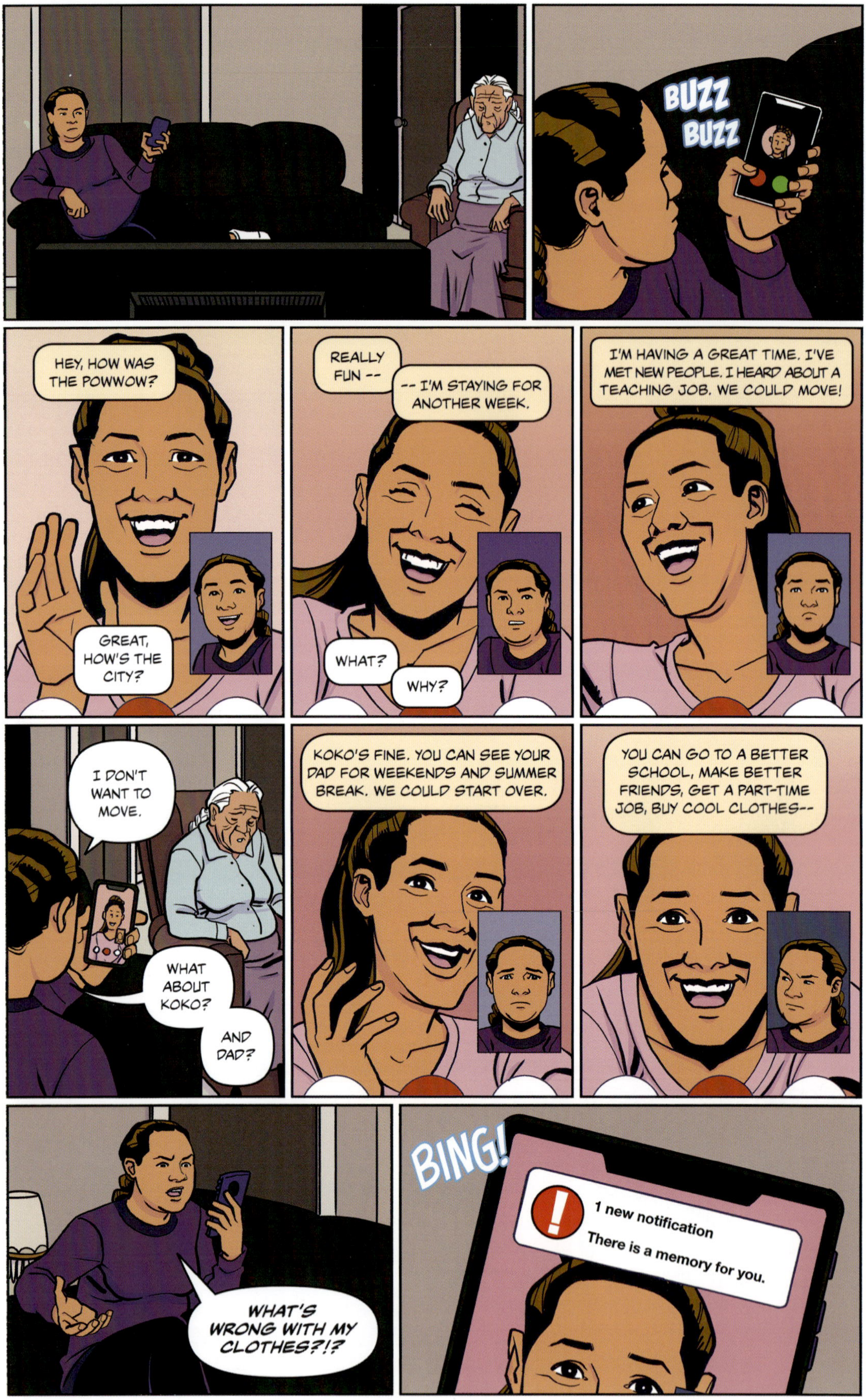
BUZZ
BUZZ
HEY, HOW WAS THE POWWOW?
GREAT, HOW'S THE CITY?
REALLY FUN --
-- I'M STAYING FOR ANOTHER WEEK.
WHAT?
WHY?
I'M HAVING A GREAT TIME. I'VE MET NEW PEOPLE. I HEARD ABOUT A TEACHING JOB. WE COULD MOVE!
I DON'T WANT TO MOVE.
WHAT ABOUT KOKO?
AND DAD?
KOKO'S FINE. YOU CAN SEE YOUR DAD FOR WEEKENDS AND SUMMER BREAK. WE COULD START OVER.
YOU CAN GO TO A BETTER SCHOOL, MAKE BETTER FRIENDS, GET A PART-TIME JOB, BUY COOL CLOTHES--
WHAT'S WRONG WITH MY CLOTHES?!?
BING!
1 new notification
There is a memory for you.

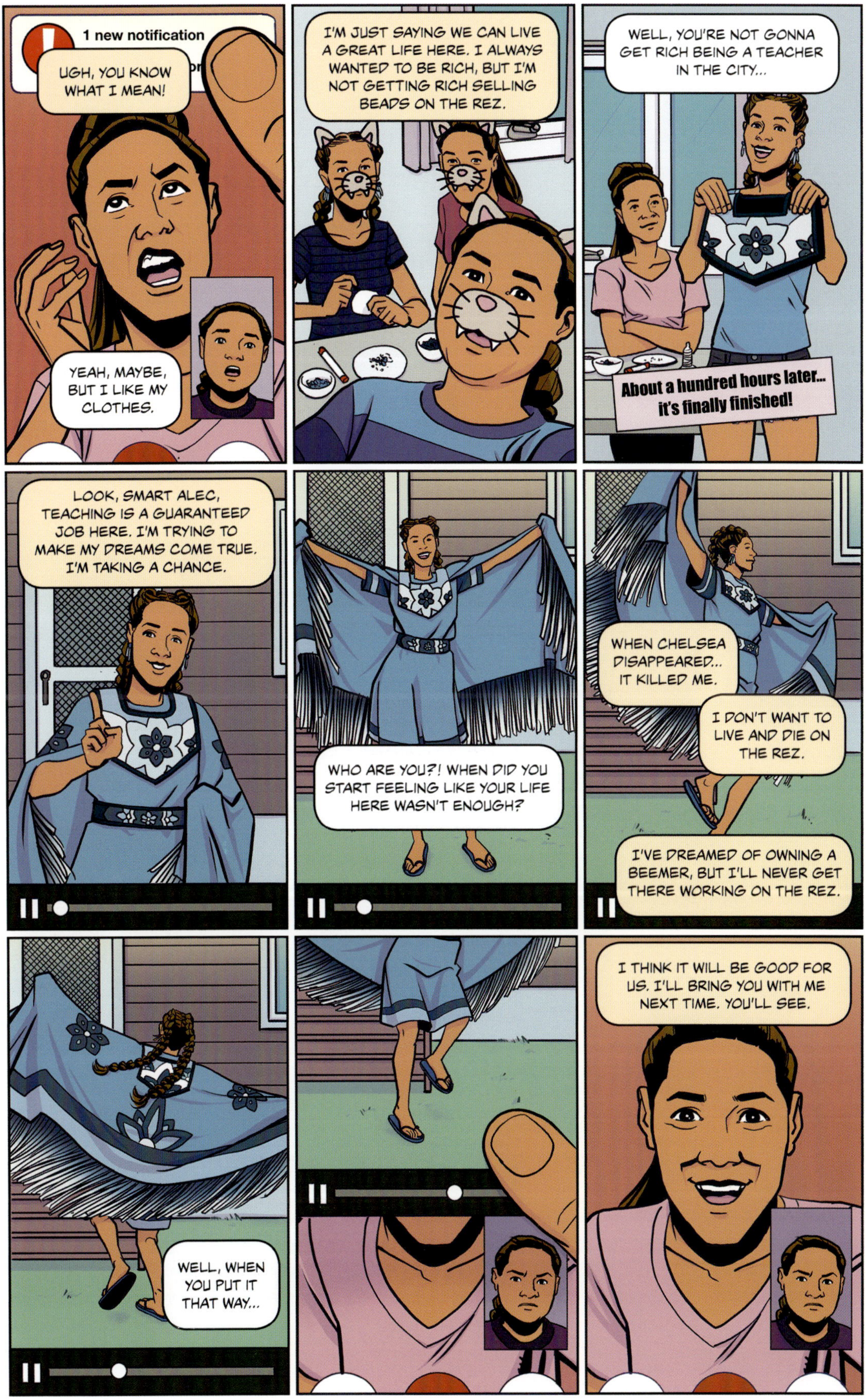
1 new notification
UGH, YOU KNOW WHAT I MEAN!
YEAH, MAYBE, BUT I LIKE MY CLOTHES.
I'M JUST SAYING WE CAN LIVE A GREAT LIFE HERE. I ALWAYS WANTED TO BE RICH, BUT I'M NOT GETTING RICH SELLING BEADS ON THE REZ.
WELL, YOU'RE NOT GONNA GET RICH BEING A TEACHER IN THE CITY...
About a hundred hours later... it's finally finished!
LOOK, SMART ALEC, TEACHING IS A GUARANTEED JOB HERE. I'M TRYING TO MAKE MY DREAMS COME TRUE. I'M TAKING A CHANCE.
WHO ARE YOU?! WHEN DID YOU START FEELING LIKE YOUR LIFE HERE WASN'T ENOUGH?
WHEN CHELSEA DISAPPEARED... IT KILLED ME.
I DON'T WANT TO LIVE AND DIE ON THE REZ.
I'VE DREAMED OF OWNING A BEEMER, BUT I'LL NEVER GET THERE WORKING ON THE REZ.
WELL, WHEN YOU PUT IT THAT WAY...
I THINK IT WILL BE GOOD FOR US. I'LL BRING YOU WITH ME NEXT TIME. YOU'LL SEE.

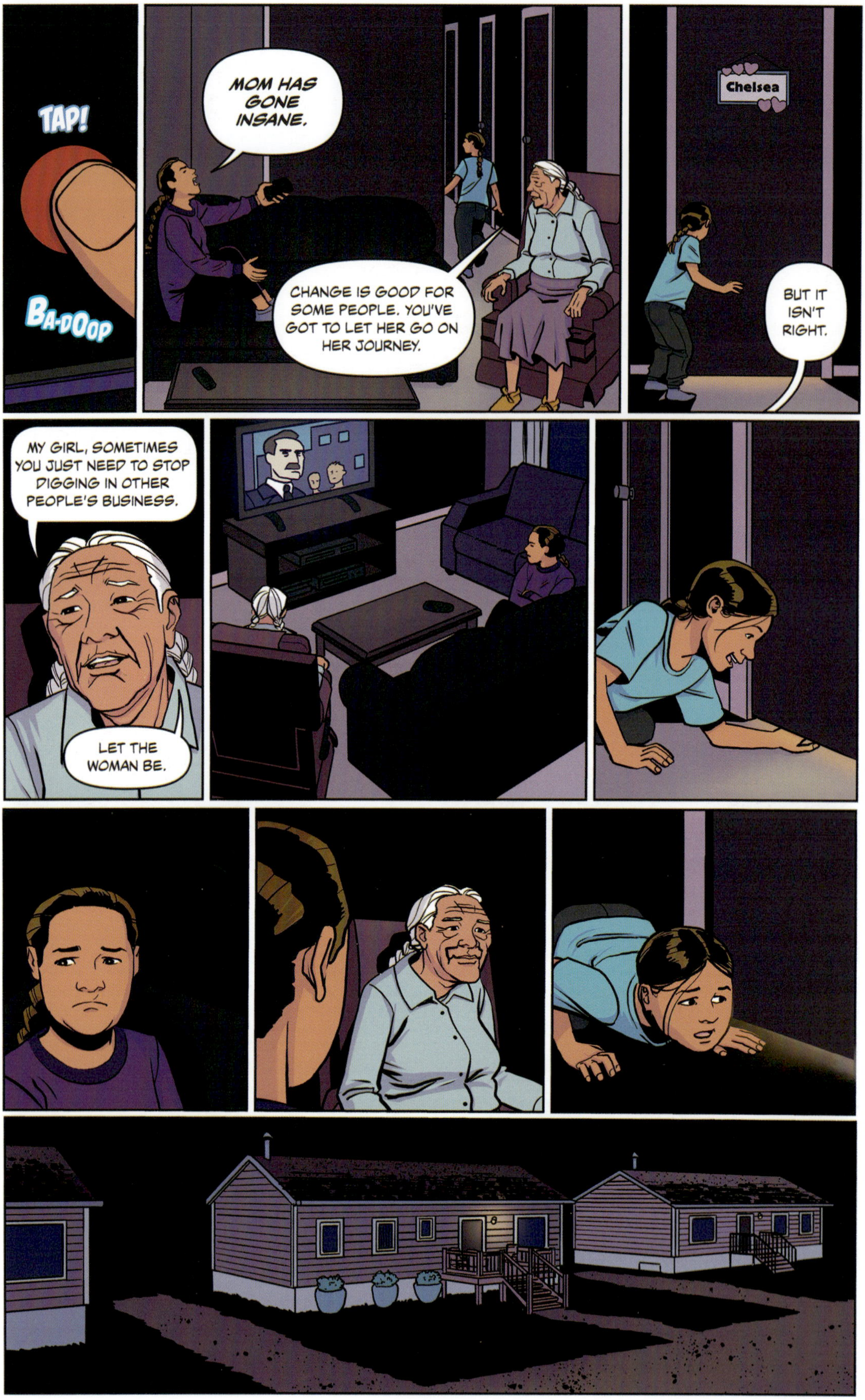
TAP!
BA-DOOP
MOM HAS GONE INSANE.
CHANGE IS GOOD FOR SOME PEOPLE. YOU'VE GOT TO LET HER GO ON HER JOURNEY.
Chelsea
BUT IT ISN'T RIGHT.
MY GIRL, SOMETIMES YOU JUST NEED TO STOP DIGGING IN OTHER PEOPLE'S BUSINESS.
LET THE WOMAN BE.

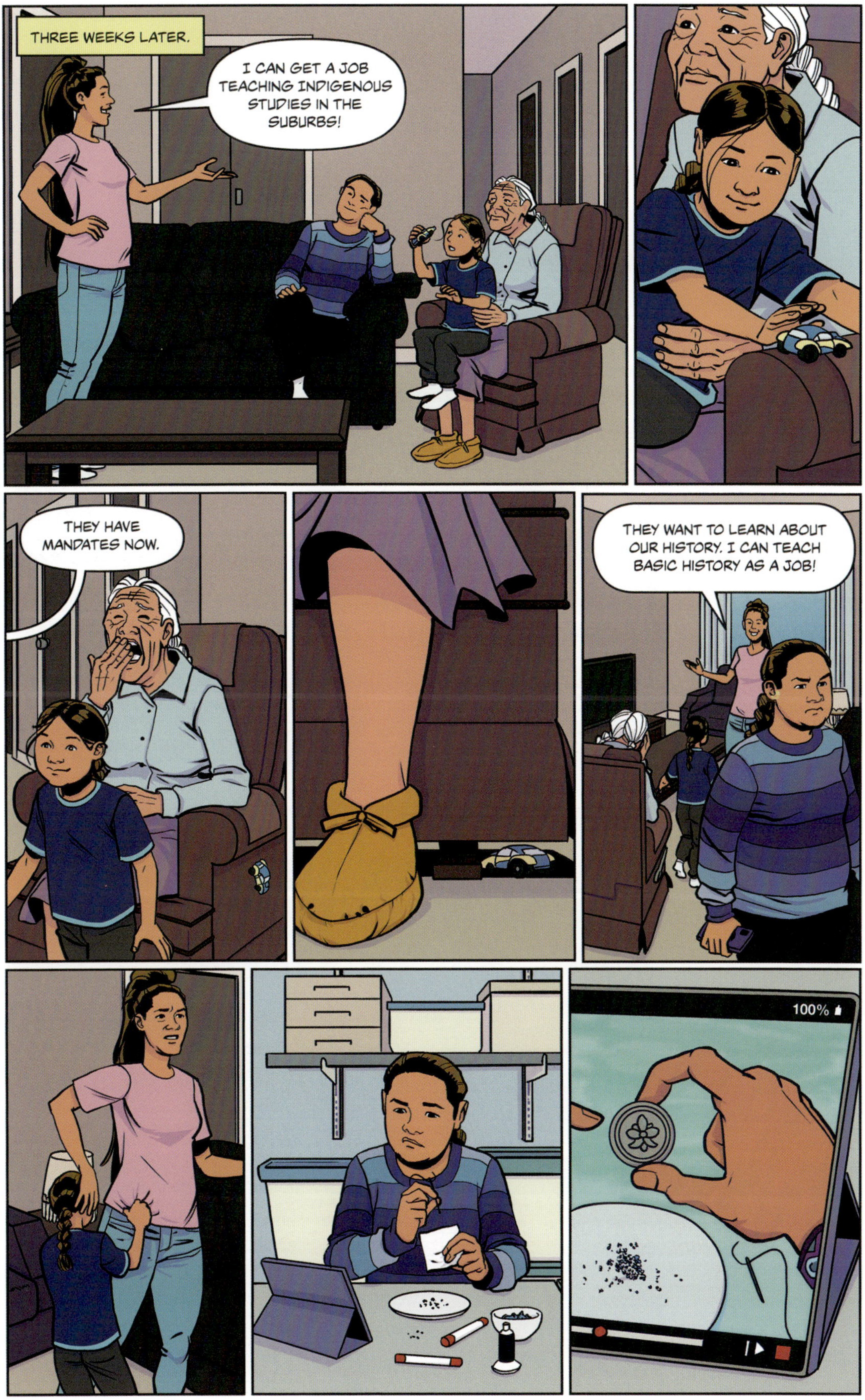
THREE WEEKS LATER.
I CAN GET A JOB TEACHING INDIGENOUS STUDIES IN THE SUBURBS!
THEY HAVE MANDATES NOW.
THEY WANT TO LEARN ABOUT OUR HISTORY. I CAN TEACH BASIC HISTORY AS A JOB!
100%

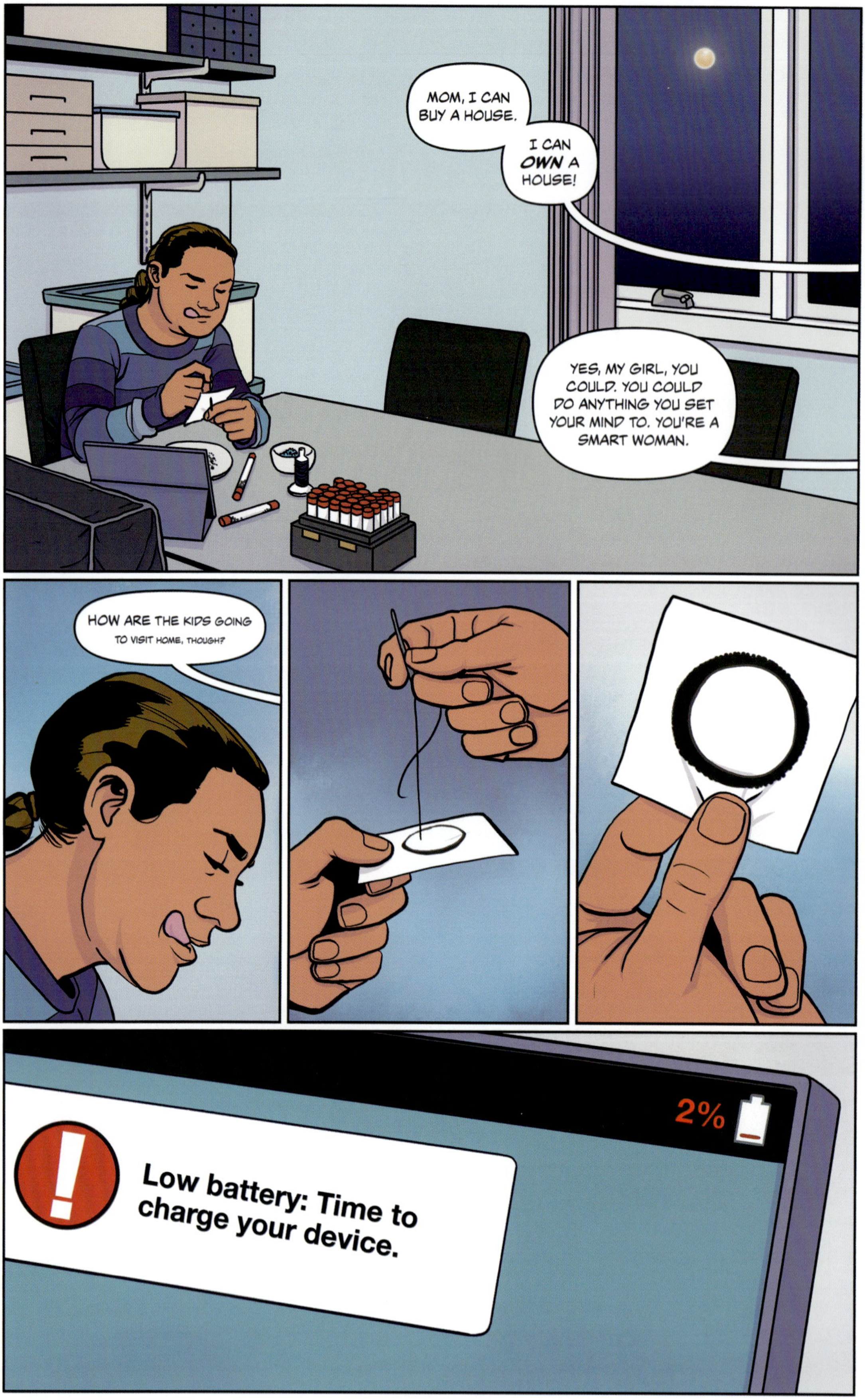
MOM, I CAN BUY A HOUSE.
I CAN OWN A HOUSE!
YES, MY GIRL, YOU COULD. YOU COULD DO ANYTHING YOU SET YOUR MIND TO. YOU'RE A SMART WOMAN.
HOW ARE THE KIDS GOING TO VISIT HOME, THOUGH?
2%
Low battery: Time to charge your device.

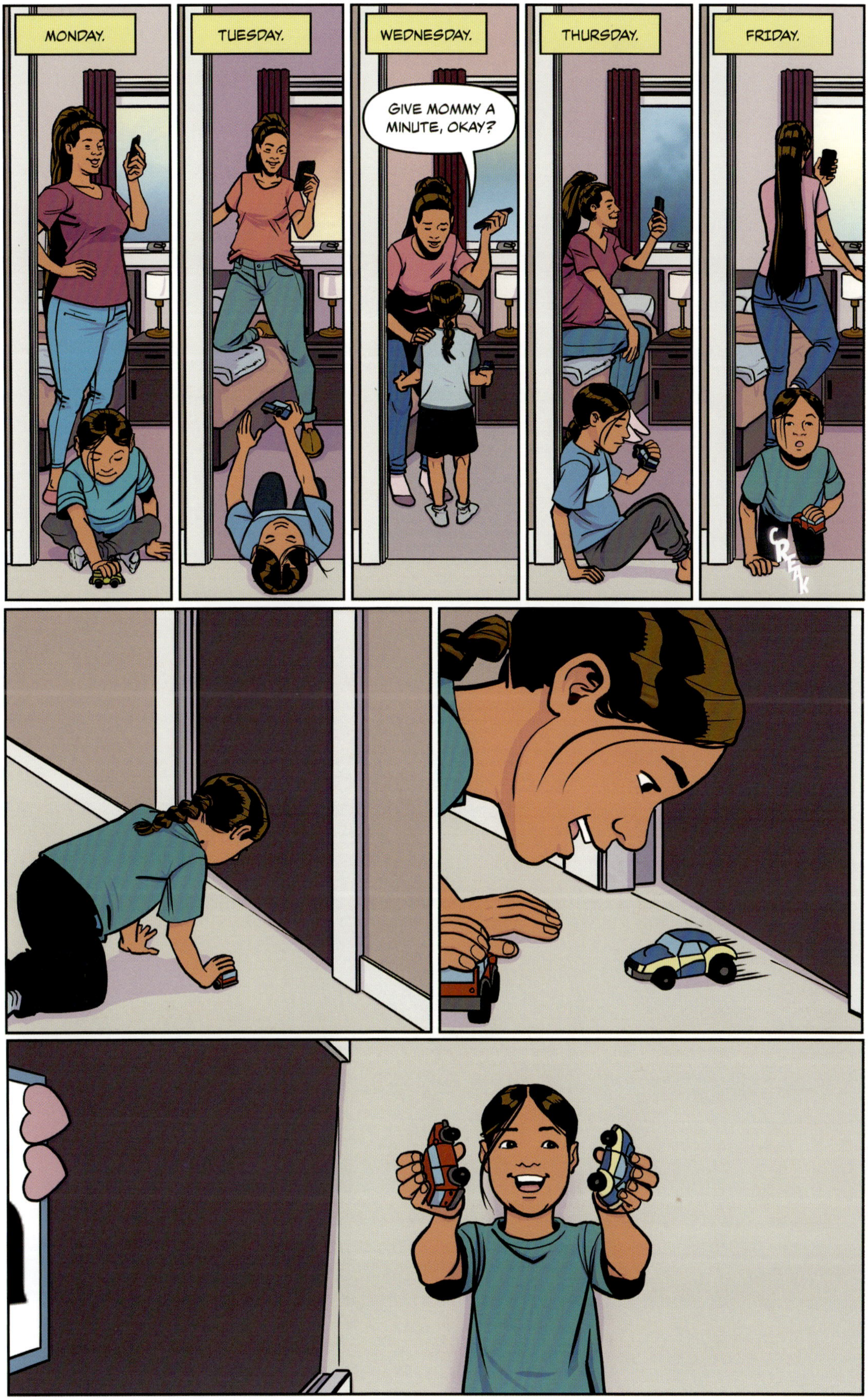
MONDAY.
TUESDAY.
WEDNESDAY.
GIVE MOMMY A MINUTE, OKAY?
THURSDAY.
FRIDAY.
CREAK

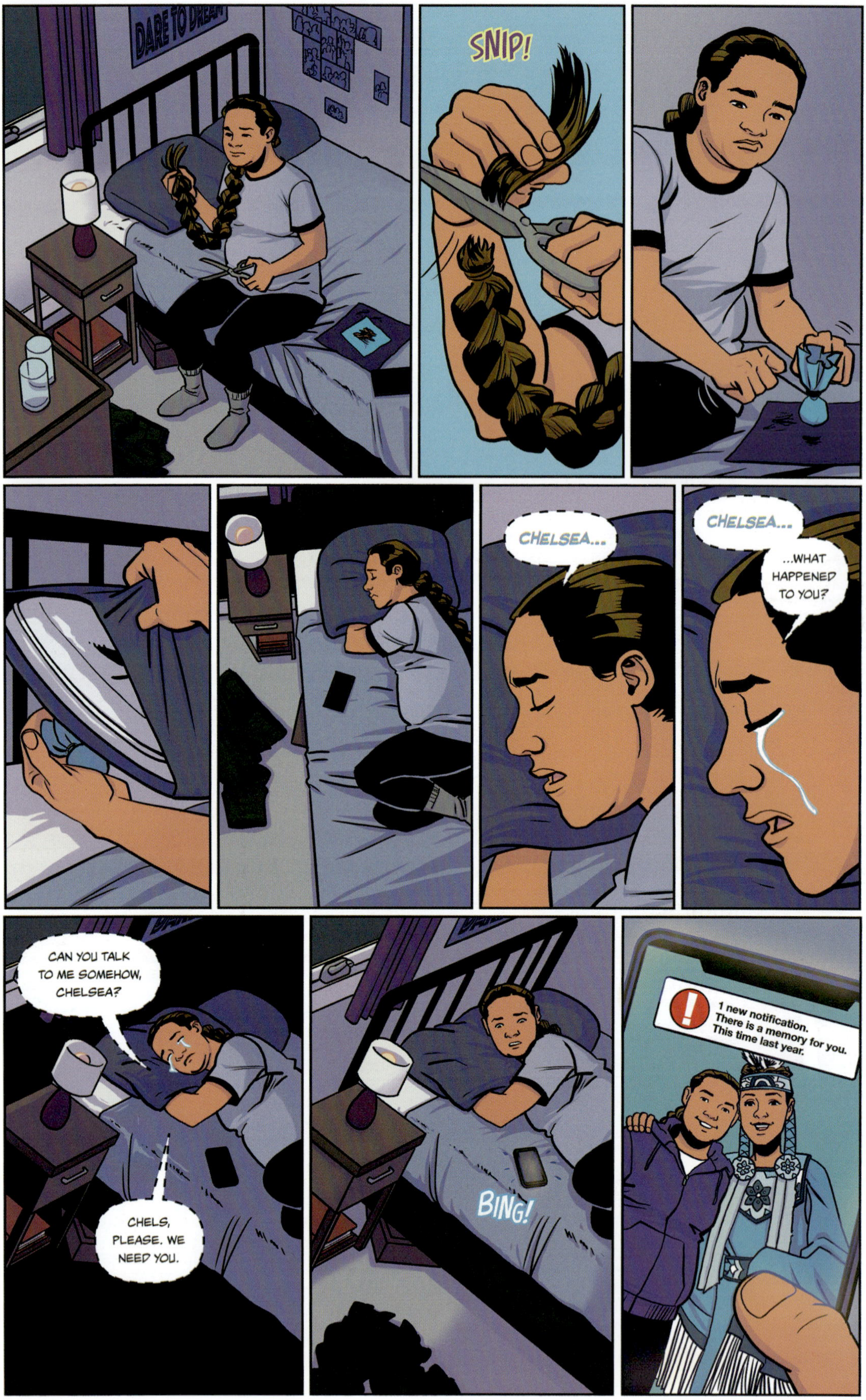
DARE TO DREAM
SNIP!
CHELSEA...
CHELSEA...
...WHAT HAPPENED TO YOU?
CAN YOU TALK TO ME SOMEHOW, CHELSEA?
CHELS, PLEASE. WE NEED YOU.
BING!
1 new notification. There is a memory for you. This time last year.

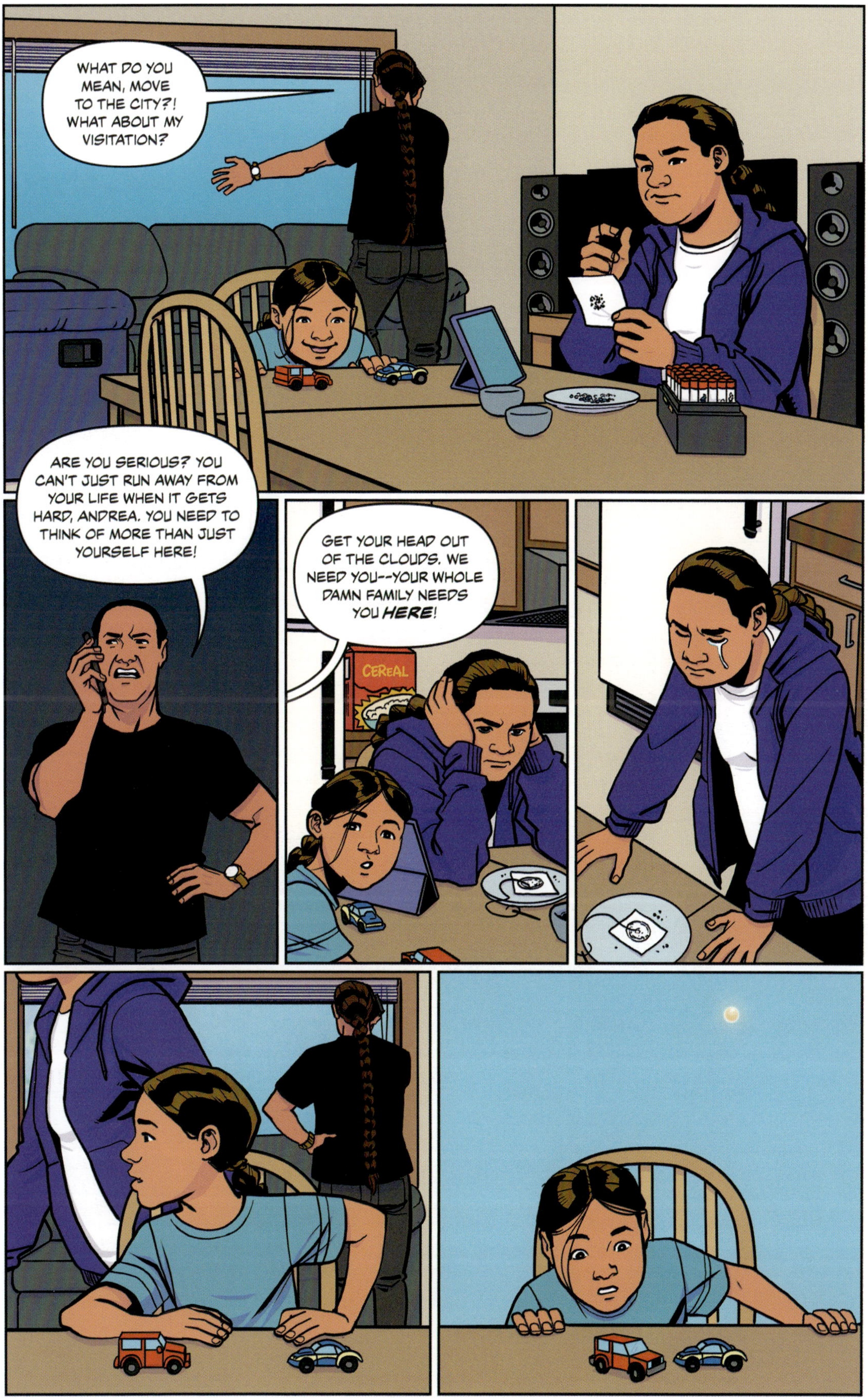
WHAT DO YOU MEAN, MOVE TO THE CITY?! WHAT ABOUT MY VISITATION?
ARE YOU SERIOUS? YOU CAN'T JUST RUN AWAY FROM YOUR LIFE WHEN IT GETS HARD, ANDREA. YOU NEED TO THINK OF MORE THAN JUST YOURSELF HERE!
GET YOUR HEAD OUT OF THE CLOUDS. WE NEED YOU--YOUR WHOLE DAMN FAMILY NEEDS YOU **HERE**!
CEREAL

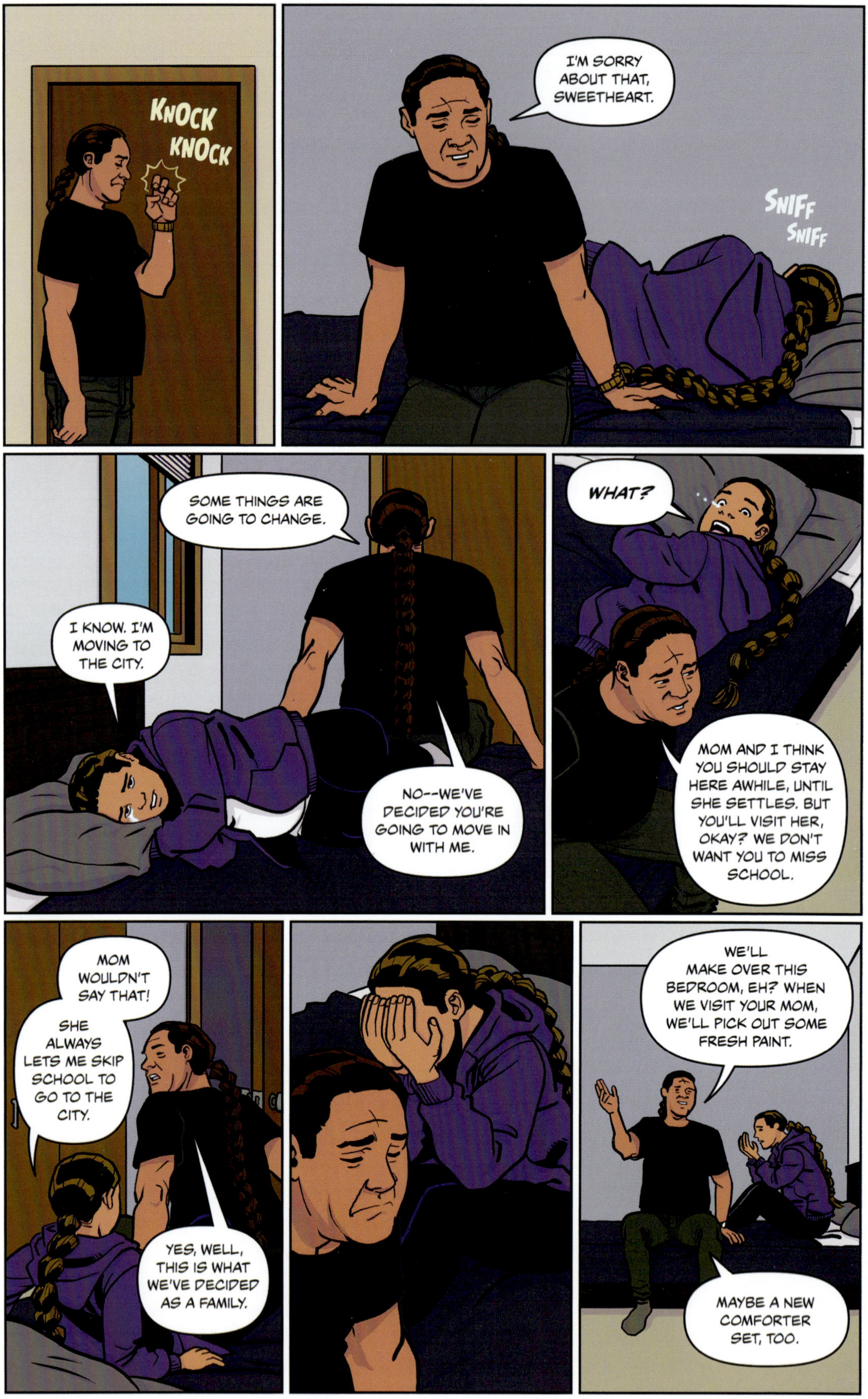
KNOCK KNOCK
I'M SORRY ABOUT THAT, SWEETHEART.
SNIFF SNIFF
SOME THINGS ARE GOING TO CHANGE.
I KNOW. I'M MOVING TO THE CITY.
NO--WE'VE DECIDED YOU'RE GOING TO MOVE IN WITH ME.
WHAT?
MOM AND I THINK YOU SHOULD STAY HERE AWHILE, UNTIL SHE SETTLES. BUT YOU'LL VISIT HER, OKAY? WE DON'T WANT YOU TO MISS SCHOOL.
MOM WOULDN'T SAY THAT!
SHE ALWAYS LETS ME SKIP SCHOOL TO GO TO THE CITY.
YES, WELL, THIS IS WHAT WE'VE DECIDED AS A FAMILY.
WE'LL MAKE OVER THIS BEDROOM, EH? WHEN WE VISIT YOUR MOM, WE'LL PICK OUT SOME FRESH PAINT.
MAYBE A NEW COMFORTER SET, TOO.

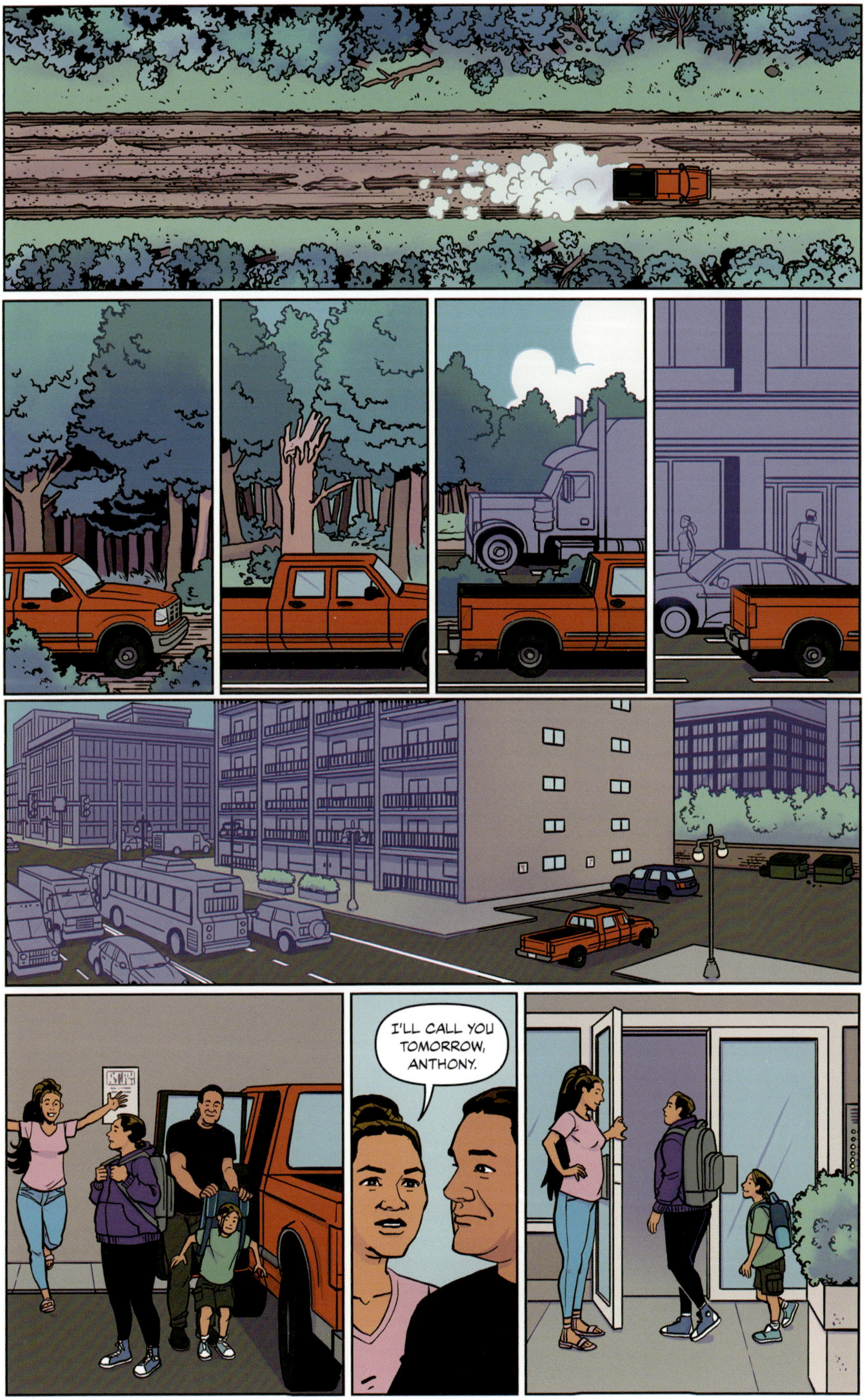
I'LL CALL YOU TOMORROW, ANTHONY.

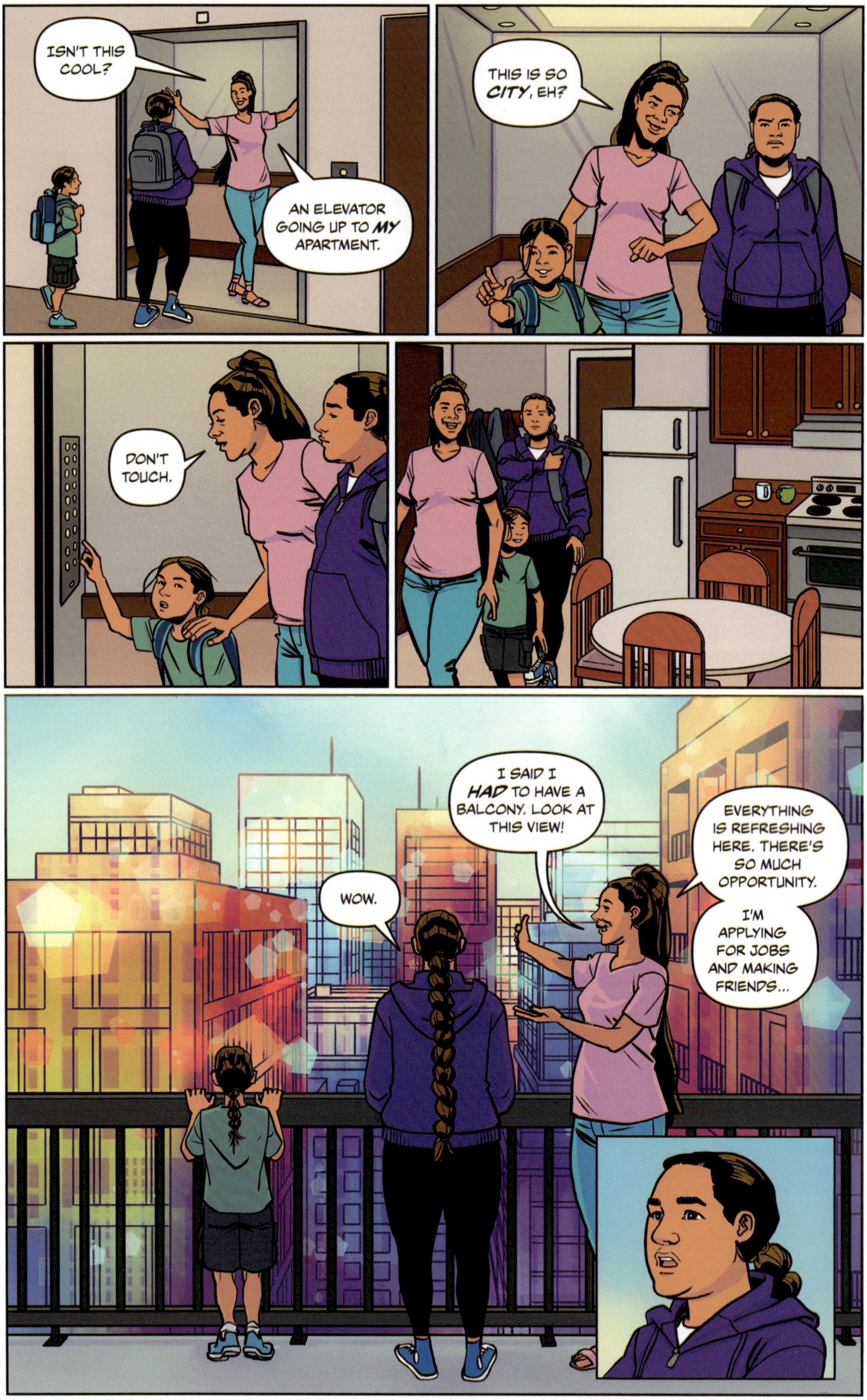
ISN'T THIS COOL?
AN ELEVATOR GOING UP TO MY APARTMENT.
THIS IS SO CITY, EH?
DON'T TOUCH.
I SAID I HAD TO HAVE A BALCONY. LOOK AT THIS VIEW!
WOW.
EVERYTHING IS REFRESHING HERE. THERE'S SO MUCH OPPORTUNITY.
I'M APPLYING FOR JOBS AND MAKING FRIENDS...

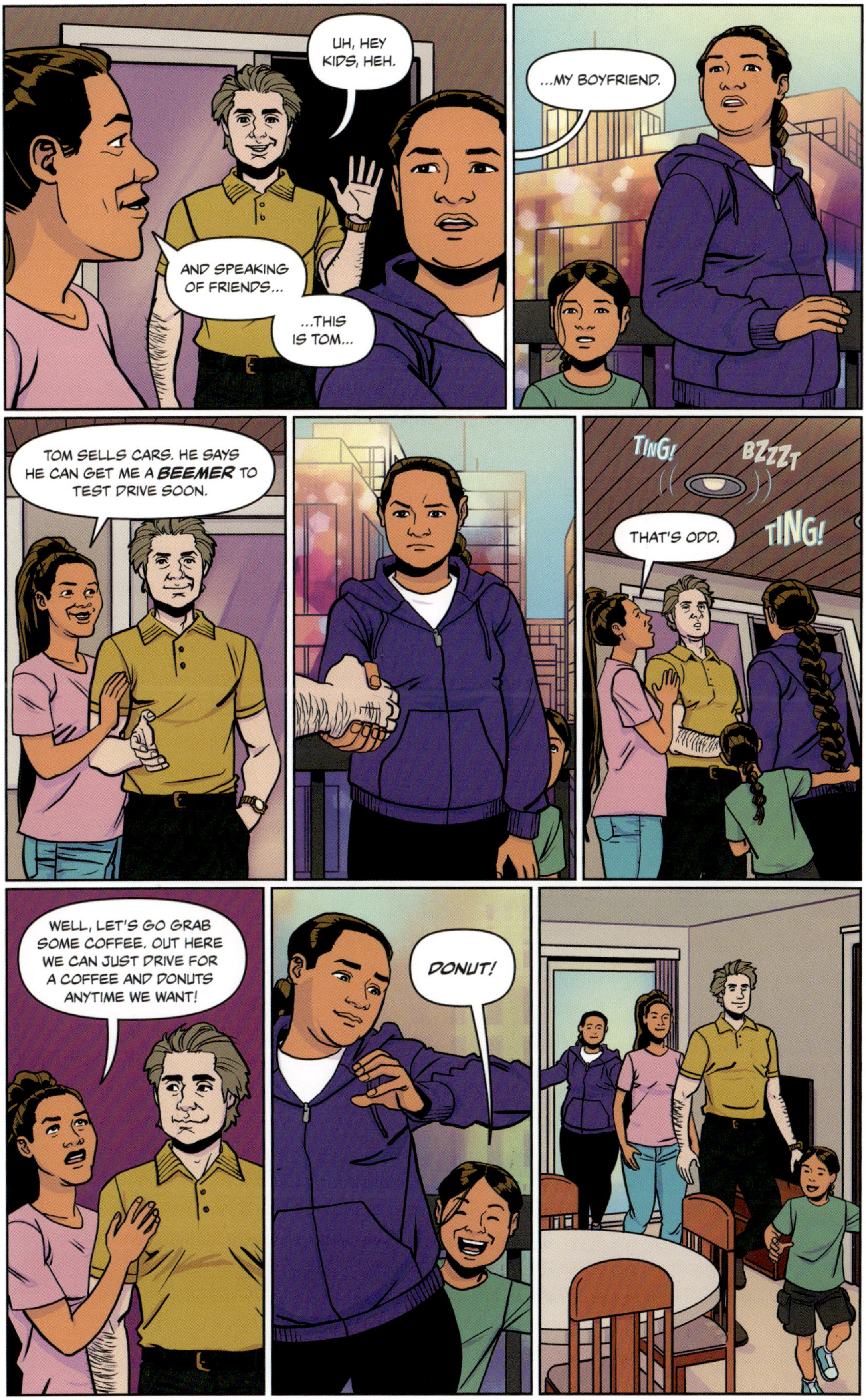
UH, HEY KIDS, HEH.
AND SPEAKING OF FRIENDS...
...THIS IS TOM...
...MY BOYFRIEND.
TOM SELLS CARS. HE SAYS HE CAN GET ME A BEEMER TO TEST DRIVE SOON.
TING!
BZZZT
TING!
THAT'S ODD.
WELL, LET'S GO GRAB SOME COFFEE. OUT HERE WE CAN JUST DRIVE FOR A COFFEE AND DONUTS ANYTIME WE WANT!
DONUT!

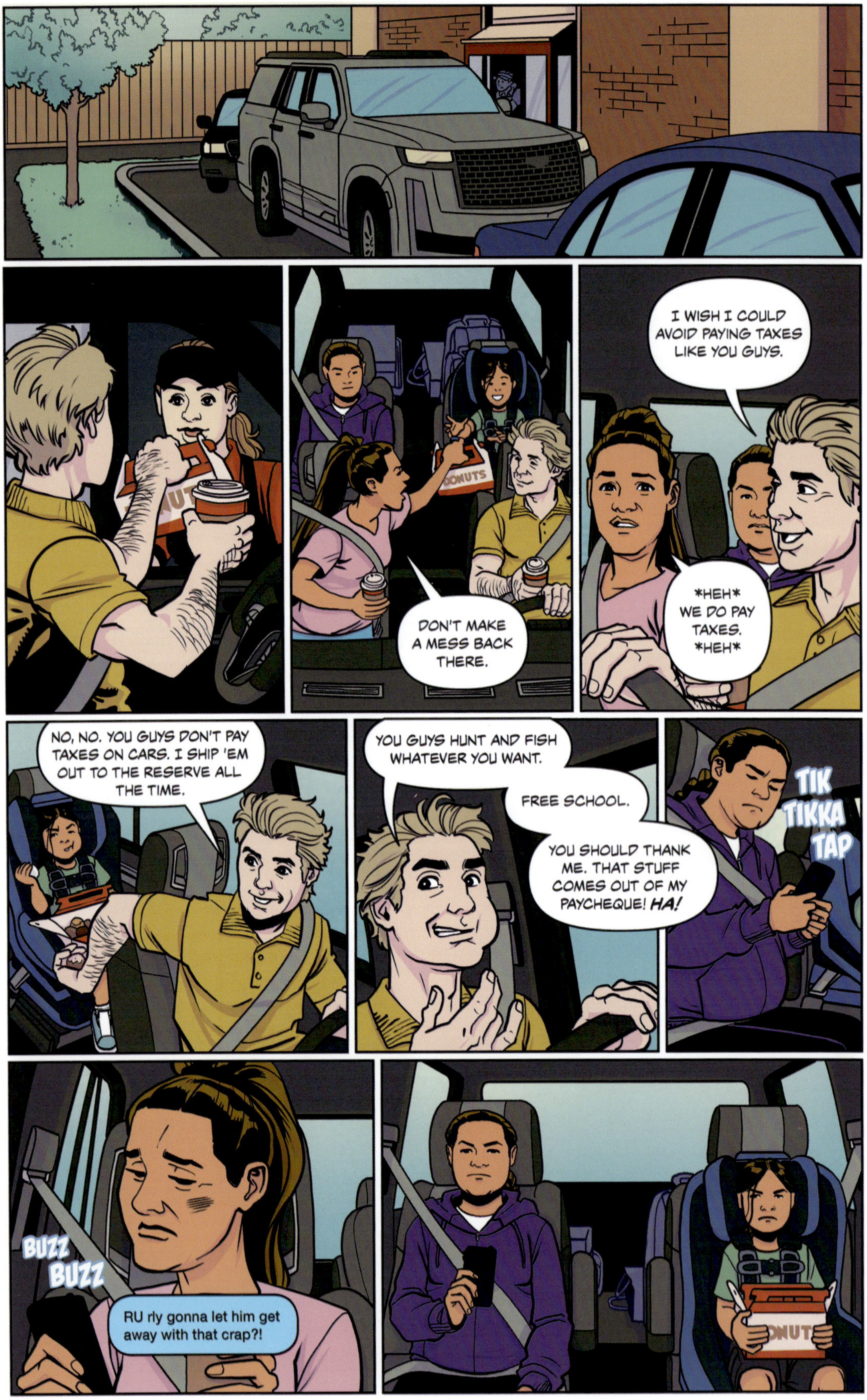

DONUTS
DON'T MAKE A MESS BACK THERE.
I WISH I COULD AVOID PAYING TAXES LIKE YOU GUYS.
HEH WE DO PAY TAXES. *HEH*
NO, NO. YOU GUYS DON'T PAY TAXES ON CARS. I SHIP 'EM OUT TO THE RESERVE ALL THE TIME.
YOU GUYS HUNT AND FISH WHATEVER YOU WANT.
FREE SCHOOL.
YOU SHOULD THANK ME. THAT STUFF COMES OUT OF MY PAYCHEQUE! HA!
TIK TIKKA TAP
BUZZ BUZZ
RU rly gonna let him get away with that crap?!

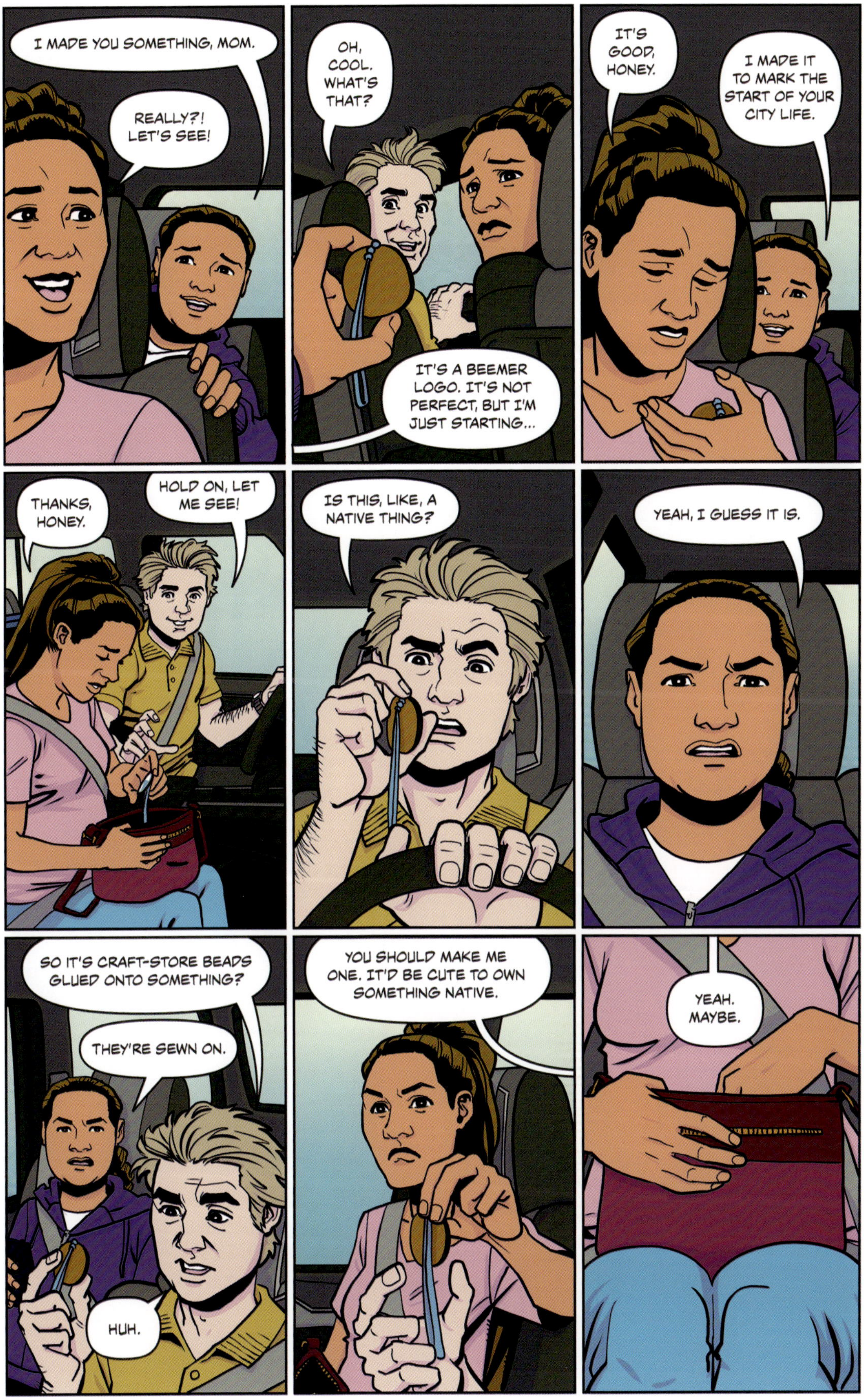
I MADE YOU SOMETHING, MOM.
REALLY?! LET'S SEE!
OH, COOL. WHAT'S THAT?
IT'S A BEEMER LOGO. IT'S NOT PERFECT, BUT I'M JUST STARTING...
IT'S GOOD, HONEY.
I MADE IT TO MARK THE START OF YOUR CITY LIFE.
THANKS, HONEY.
HOLD ON, LET ME SEE!
IS THIS, LIKE, A NATIVE THING?
YEAH, I GUESS IT IS.
SO IT'S CRAFT-STORE BEADS GLUED ONTO SOMETHING?
THEY'RE SEWN ON.
HUH.
YOU SHOULD MAKE ME ONE. IT'D BE CUTE TO OWN SOMETHING NATIVE.
YEAH. MAYBE.

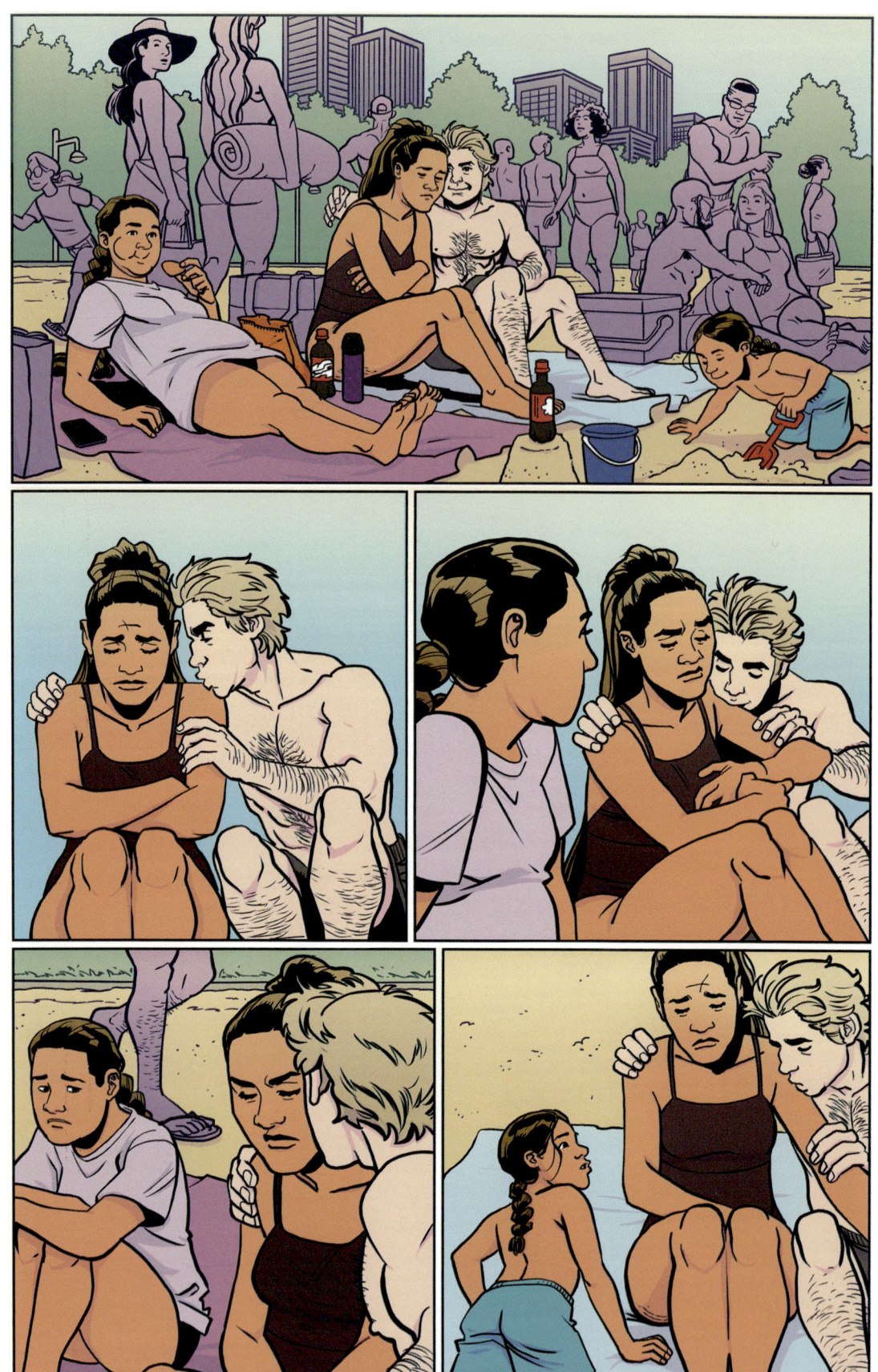

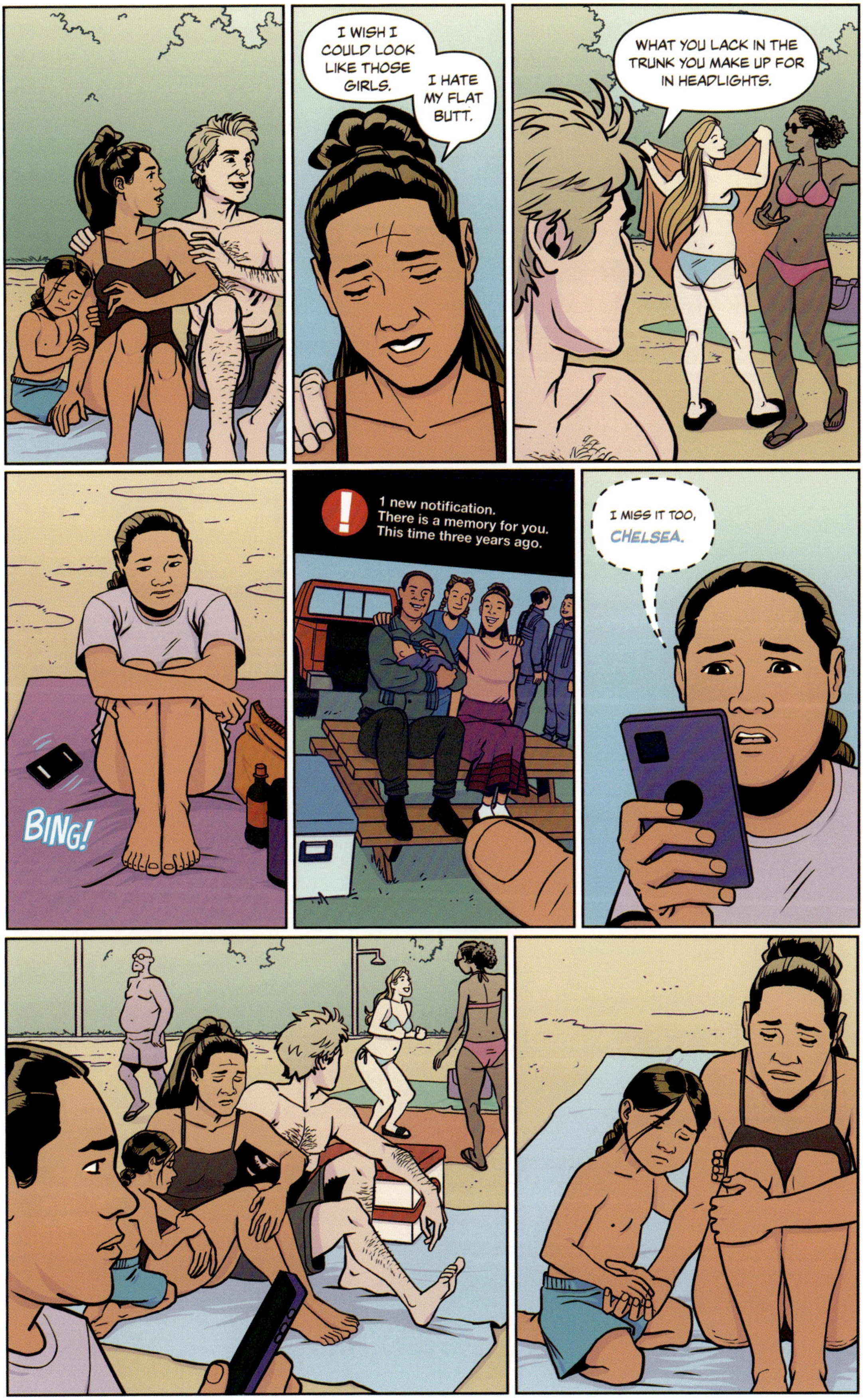
I WISH I COULD LOOK LIKE THOSE GIRLS.
I HATE MY FLAT BUTT.
WHAT YOU LACK IN THE TRUNK YOU MAKE UP FOR IN HEADLIGHTS.
BING!
1 new notification.
There is a memory for you.
This time three years ago.
I MISS IT TOO, CHELSEA.

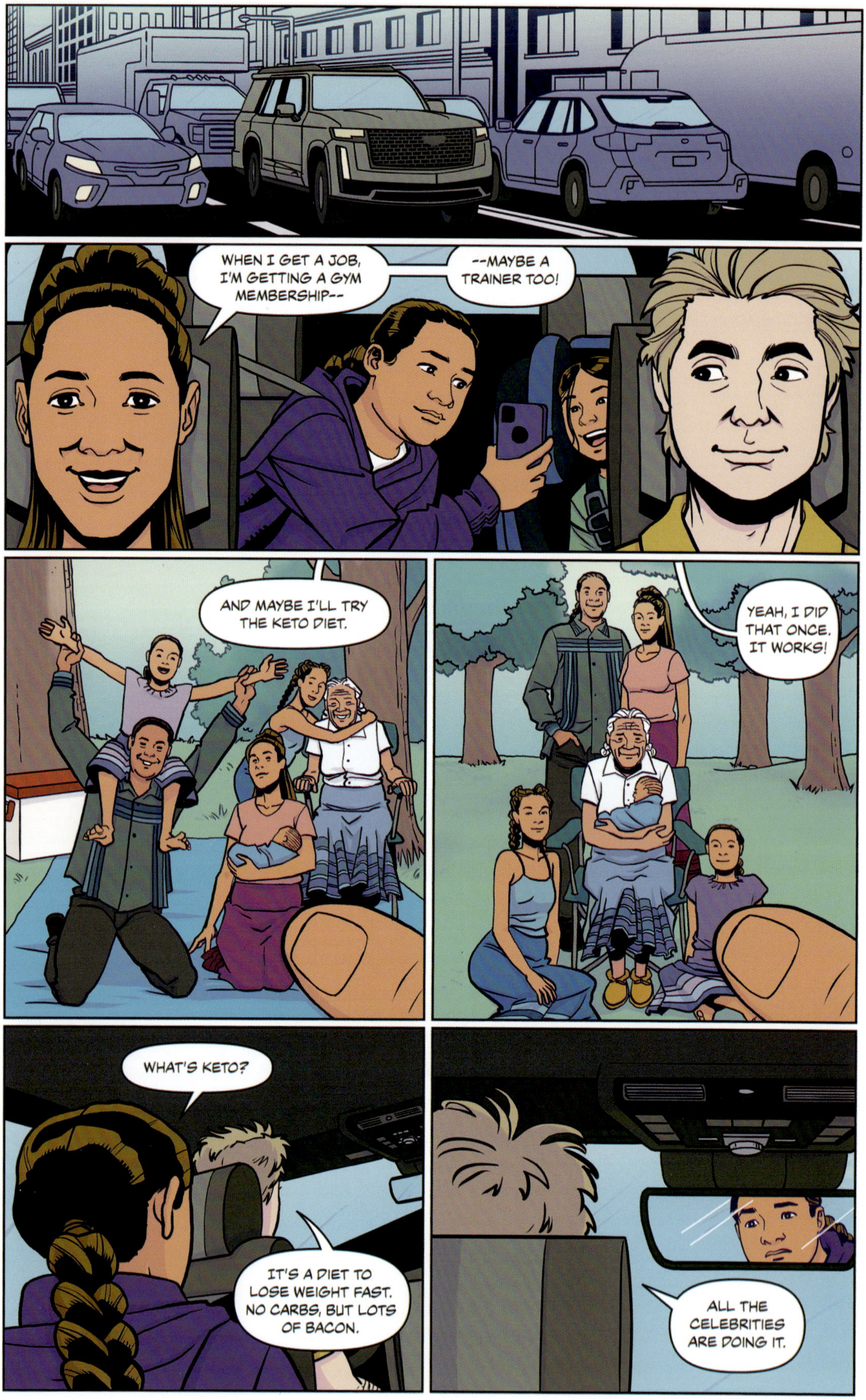
WHEN I GET A JOB, I'M GETTING A GYM MEMBERSHIP--
--MAYBE A TRAINER TOO!
AND MAYBE I'LL TRY THE KETO DIET.
YEAH, I DID THAT ONCE. IT WORKS!
WHAT'S KETO?
IT'S A DIET TO LOSE WEIGHT FAST. NO CARBS, BUT LOTS OF BACON.
ALL THE CELEBRITIES ARE DOING IT.

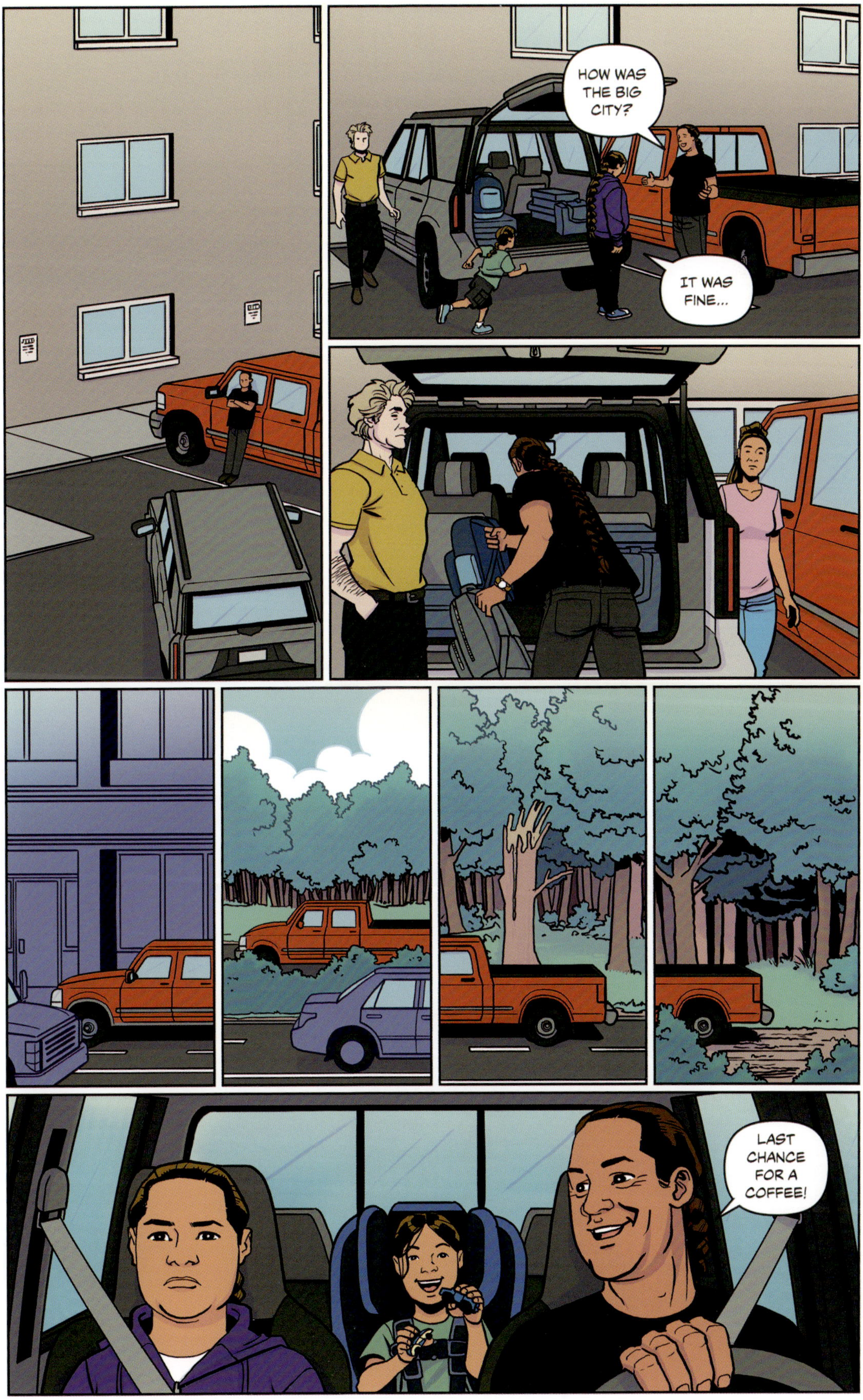
HOW WAS THE BIG CITY?
IT WAS FINE...
LAST CHANCE FOR A COFFEE!

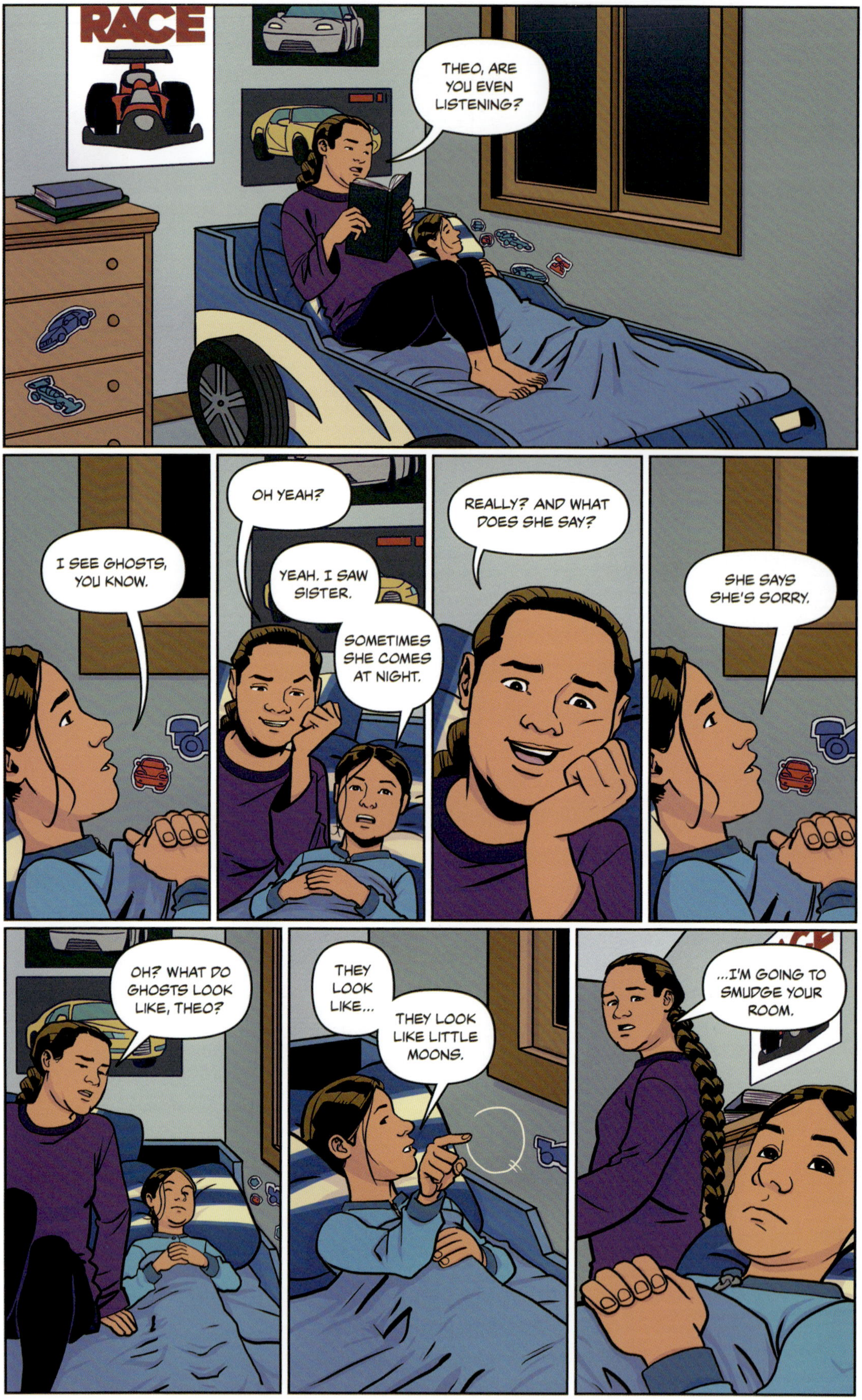
RACE
THEO, ARE YOU EVEN LISTENING?
I SEE GHOSTS, YOU KNOW.
OH YEAH?
YEAH. I SAW SISTER.
SOMETIMES SHE COMES AT NIGHT.
REALLY? AND WHAT DOES SHE SAY?
SHE SAYS SHE'S SORRY.
OH? WHAT DO GHOSTS LOOK LIKE, THEO?
THEY LOOK LIKE...
THEY LOOK LIKE LITTLE MOONS.
...I'M GOING TO SMUDGE YOUR ROOM.

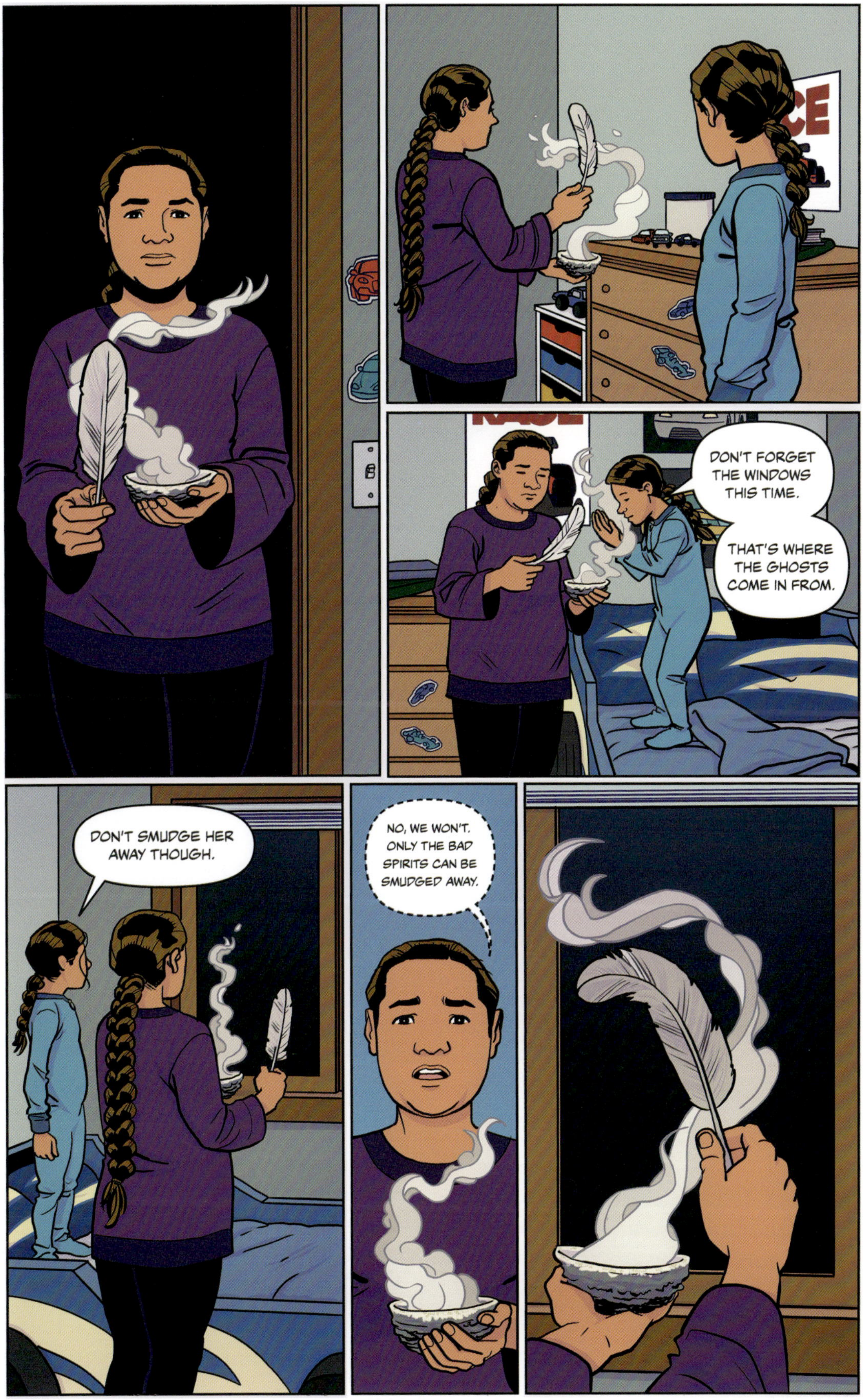
DON'T FORGET THE WINDOWS THIS TIME.
THAT'S WHERE THE GHOSTS COME IN FROM.
DON'T SMUDGE HER AWAY THOUGH.
NO, WE WON'T. ONLY THE BAD SPIRITS CAN BE SMUDGED AWAY.

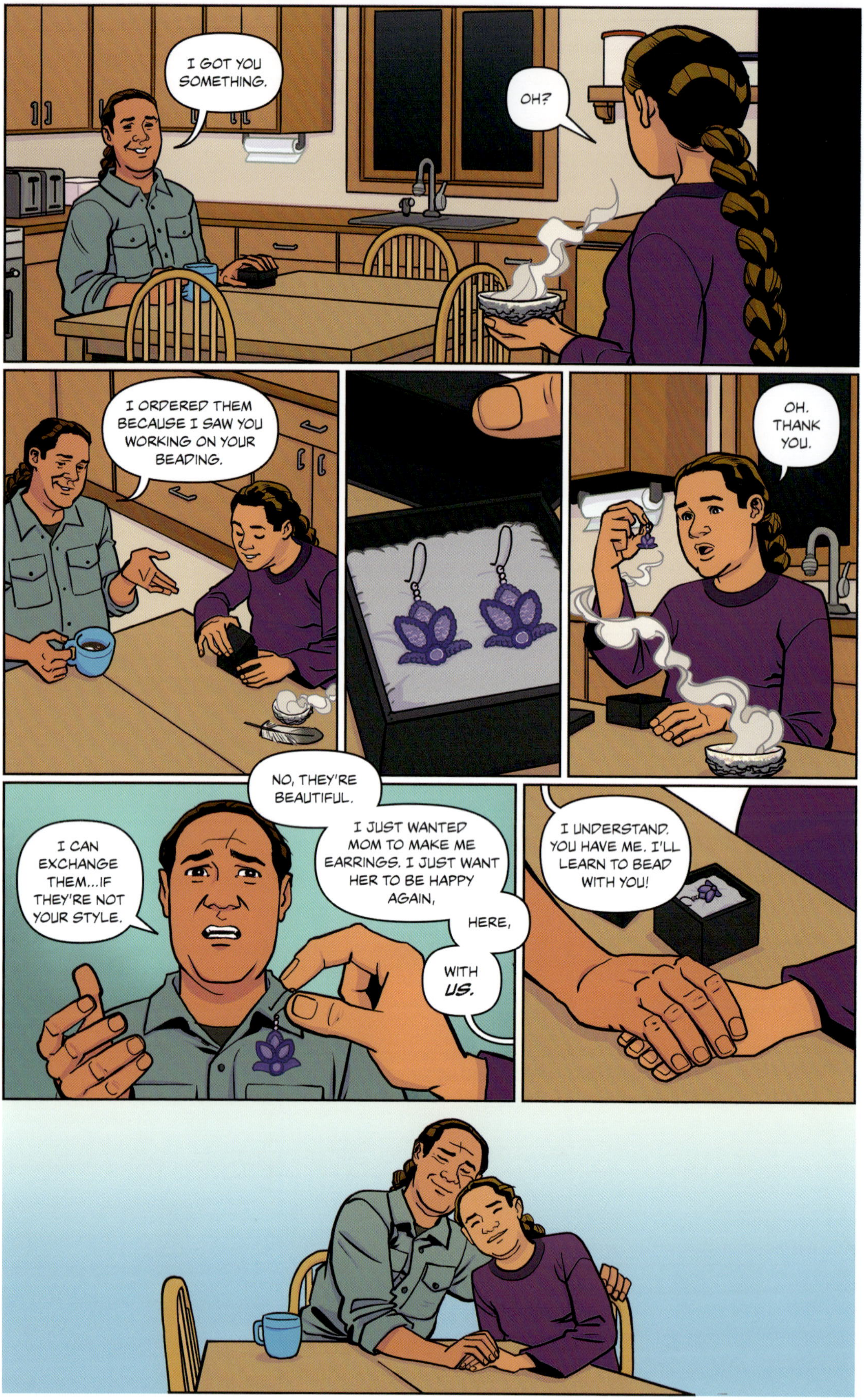
I GOT YOU SOMETHING.
OH?
I ORDERED THEM BECAUSE I SAW YOU WORKING ON YOUR BEADING.
OH. THANK YOU.
I CAN EXCHANGE THEM...IF THEY'RE NOT YOUR STYLE.
NO, THEY'RE BEAUTIFUL.
I JUST WANTED MOM TO MAKE ME EARRINGS. I JUST WANT HER TO BE HAPPY AGAIN,
HERE,
WITH *US.*
I UNDERSTAND. YOU HAVE ME. I'LL LEARN TO BEAD WITH YOU!

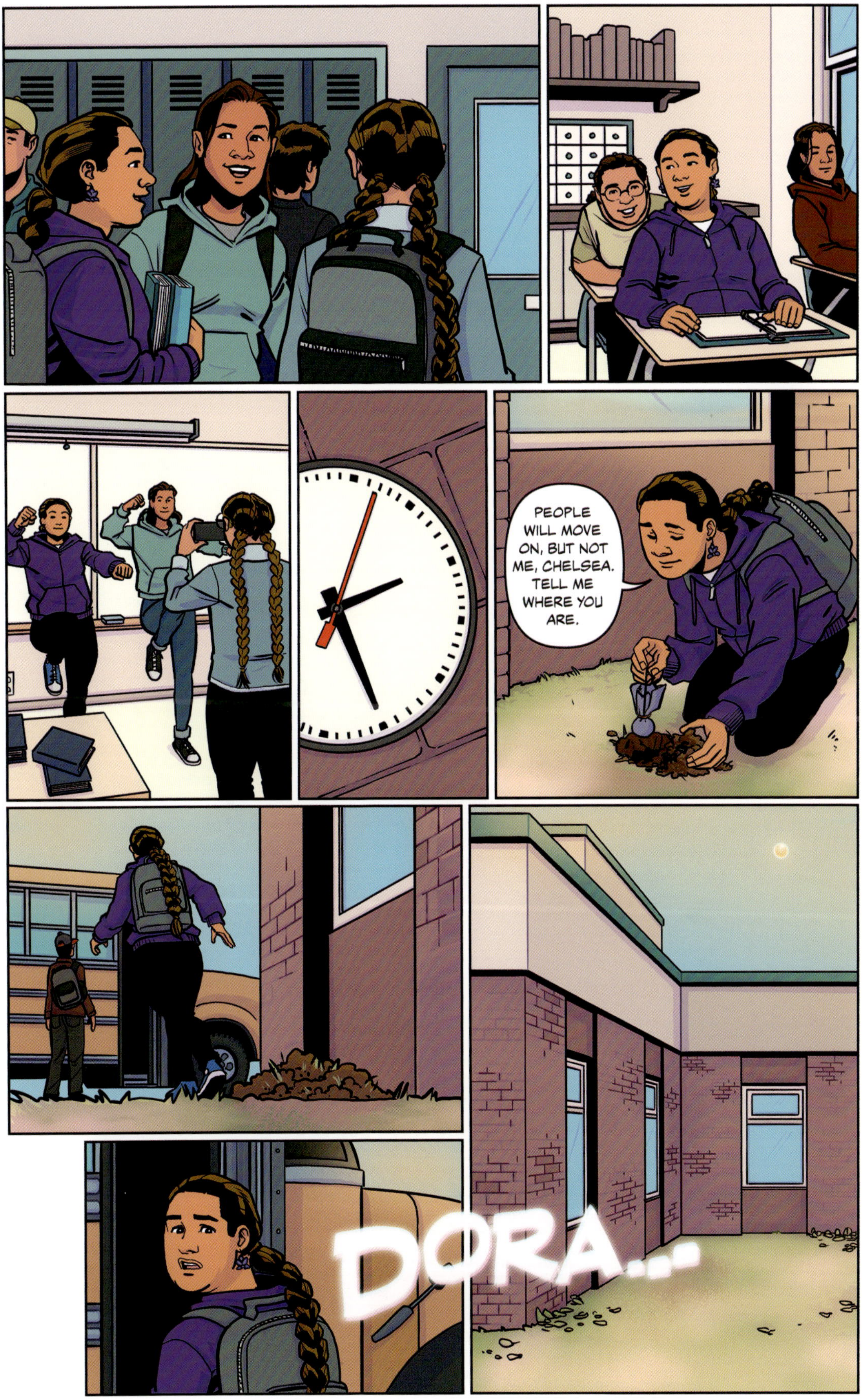
PEOPLE WILL MOVE ON, BUT NOT ME, CHELSEA. TELL ME WHERE YOU ARE.
DORA...

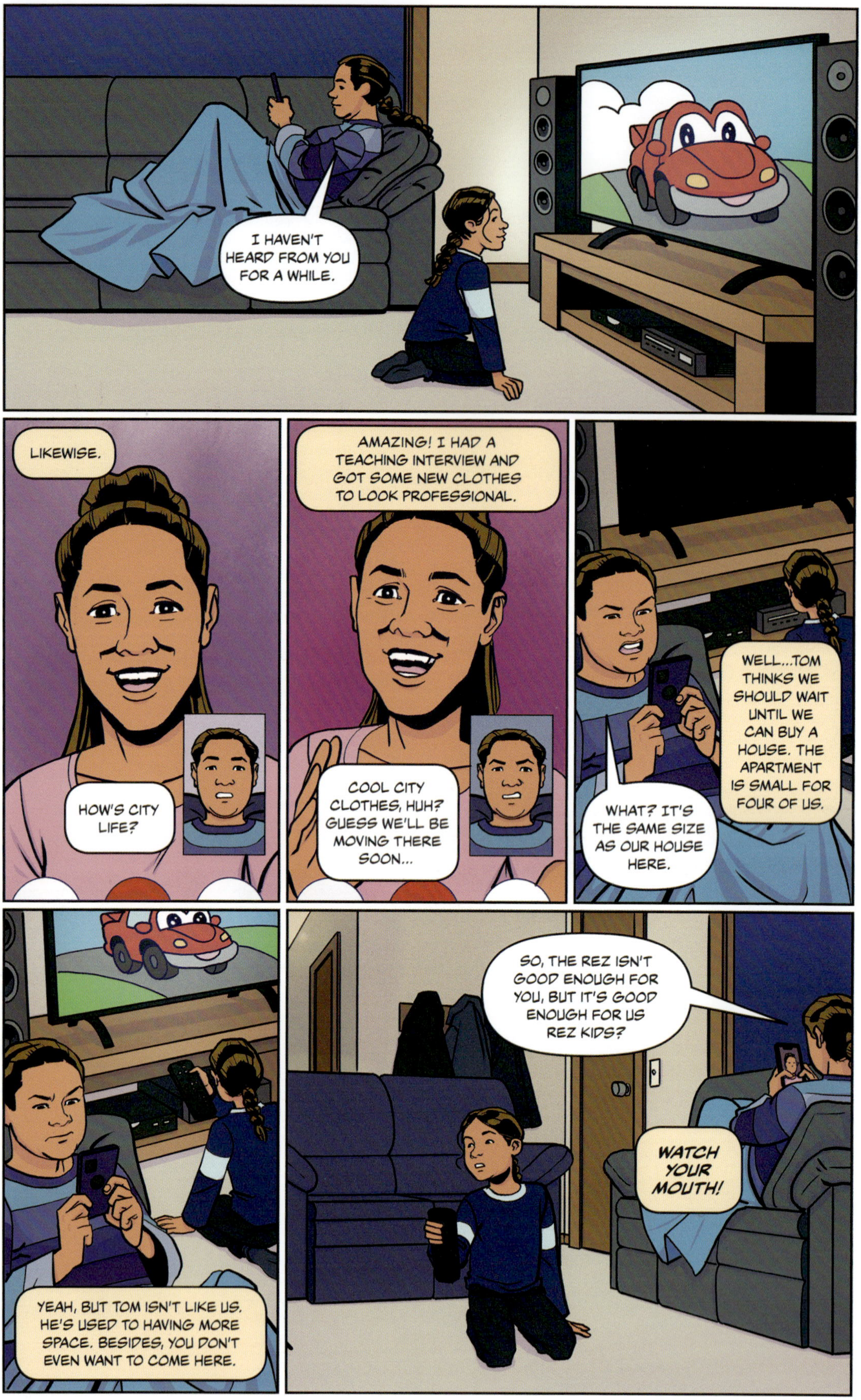
I HAVEN'T HEARD FROM YOU FOR A WHILE.
LIKEWISE.
HOW'S CITY LIFE?
AMAZING! I HAD A TEACHING INTERVIEW AND GOT SOME NEW CLOTHES TO LOOK PROFESSIONAL.
COOL CITY CLOTHES, HUH? GUESS WE'LL BE MOVING THERE SOON...
WELL...TOM THINKS WE SHOULD WAIT UNTIL WE CAN BUY A HOUSE. THE APARTMENT IS SMALL FOR FOUR OF US.
WHAT? IT'S THE SAME SIZE AS OUR HOUSE HERE.
YEAH, BUT TOM ISN'T LIKE US. HE'S USED TO HAVING MORE SPACE. BESIDES, YOU DON'T EVEN WANT TO COME HERE.
SO, THE REZ ISN'T GOOD ENOUGH FOR YOU, BUT IT'S GOOD ENOUGH FOR US REZ KIDS?
WATCH YOUR MOUTH!

WHAT? YOU CAN'T YELL AT ME ANYMORE, 'CAUSE TOM MIGHT FIND IT TOO REZZY WHEN LIFE STARTS GETTING REAL?! YOU DON'T WANT TO SCARE HIM AWAY WITH YOUR PERFECT PARENTING?
I'M SUFFOCATING! THE PAIN WON'T EVER STOP FOR ME--
BUT I HAVE TWO OTHER KIDS TO LIVE FOR.
I.
NEED.
THIS.
RACE

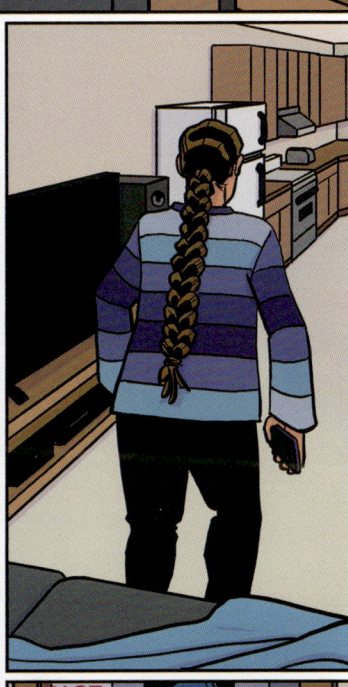

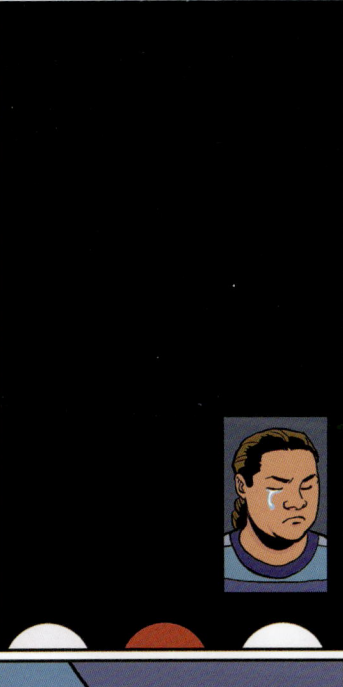

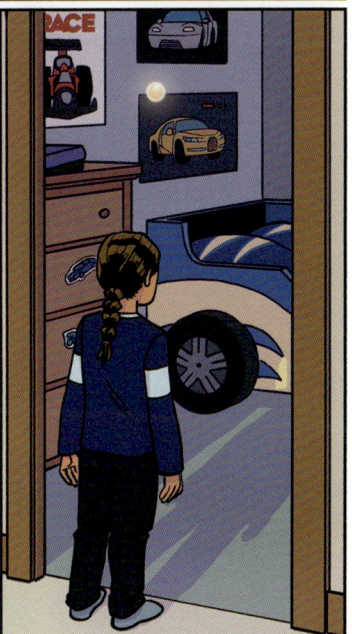

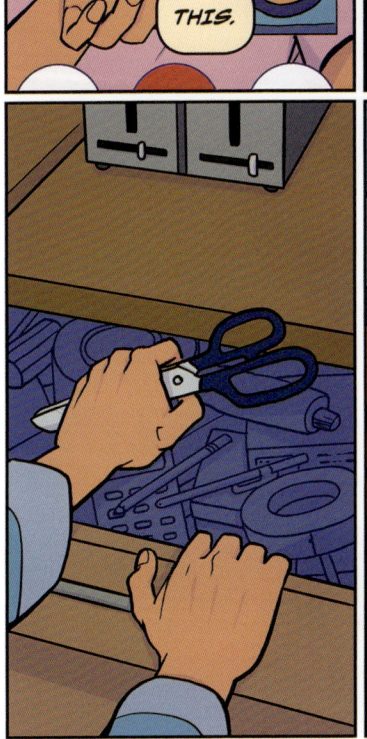

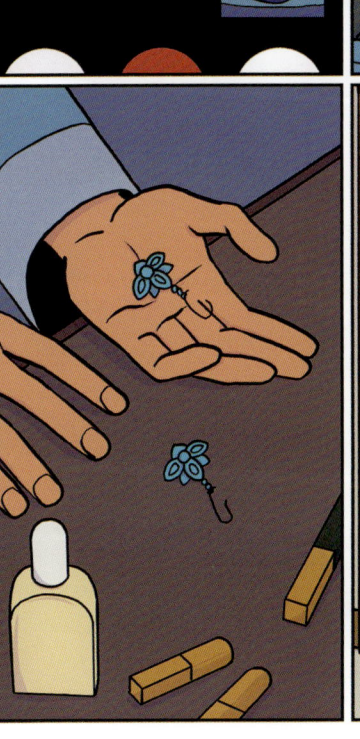

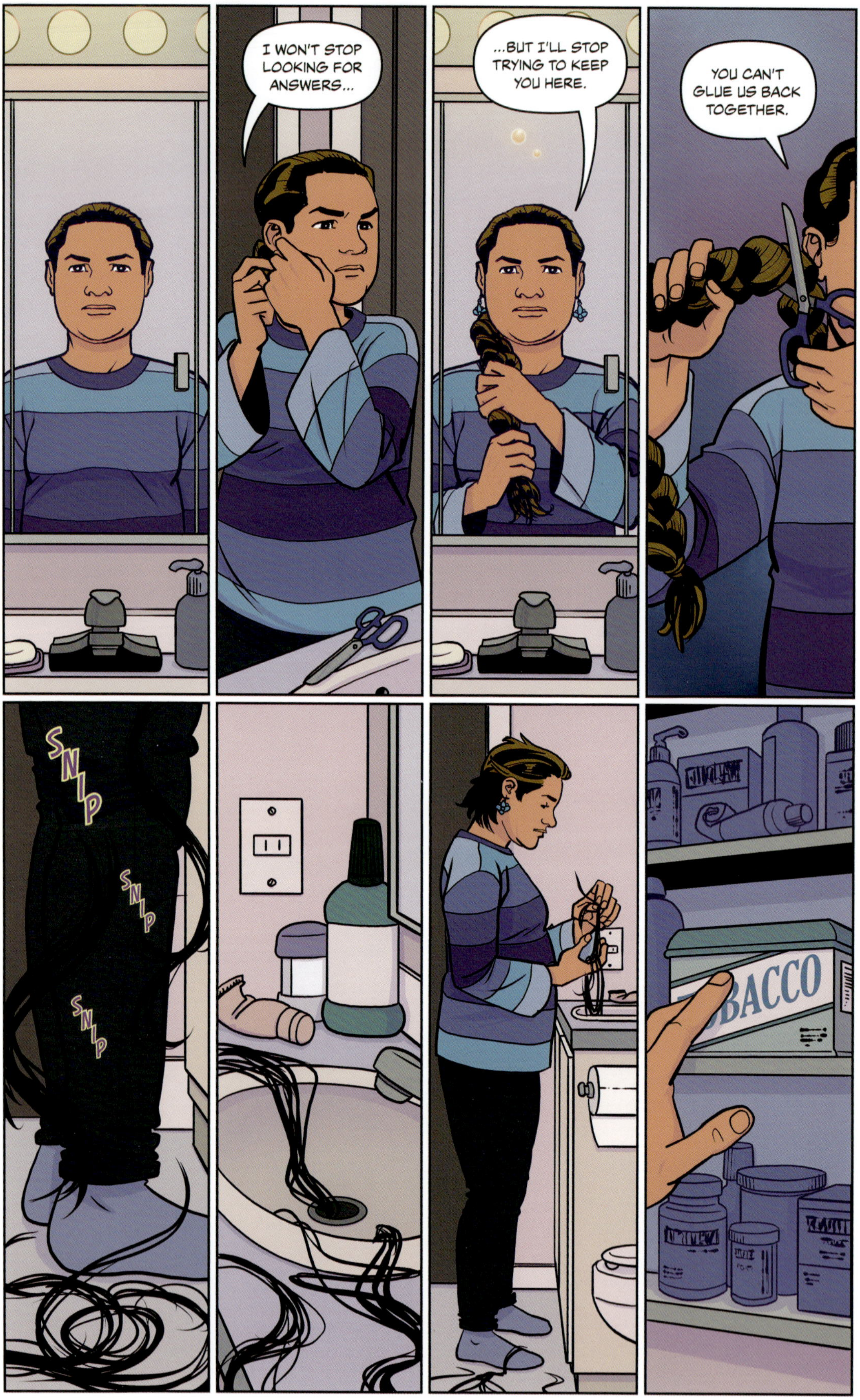
I WON'T STOP LOOKING FOR ANSWERS...
...BUT I'LL STOP TRYING TO KEEP YOU HERE.
YOU CAN'T GLUE US BACK TOGETHER.
SNIP
SNIP
SNIP
TOBACCO

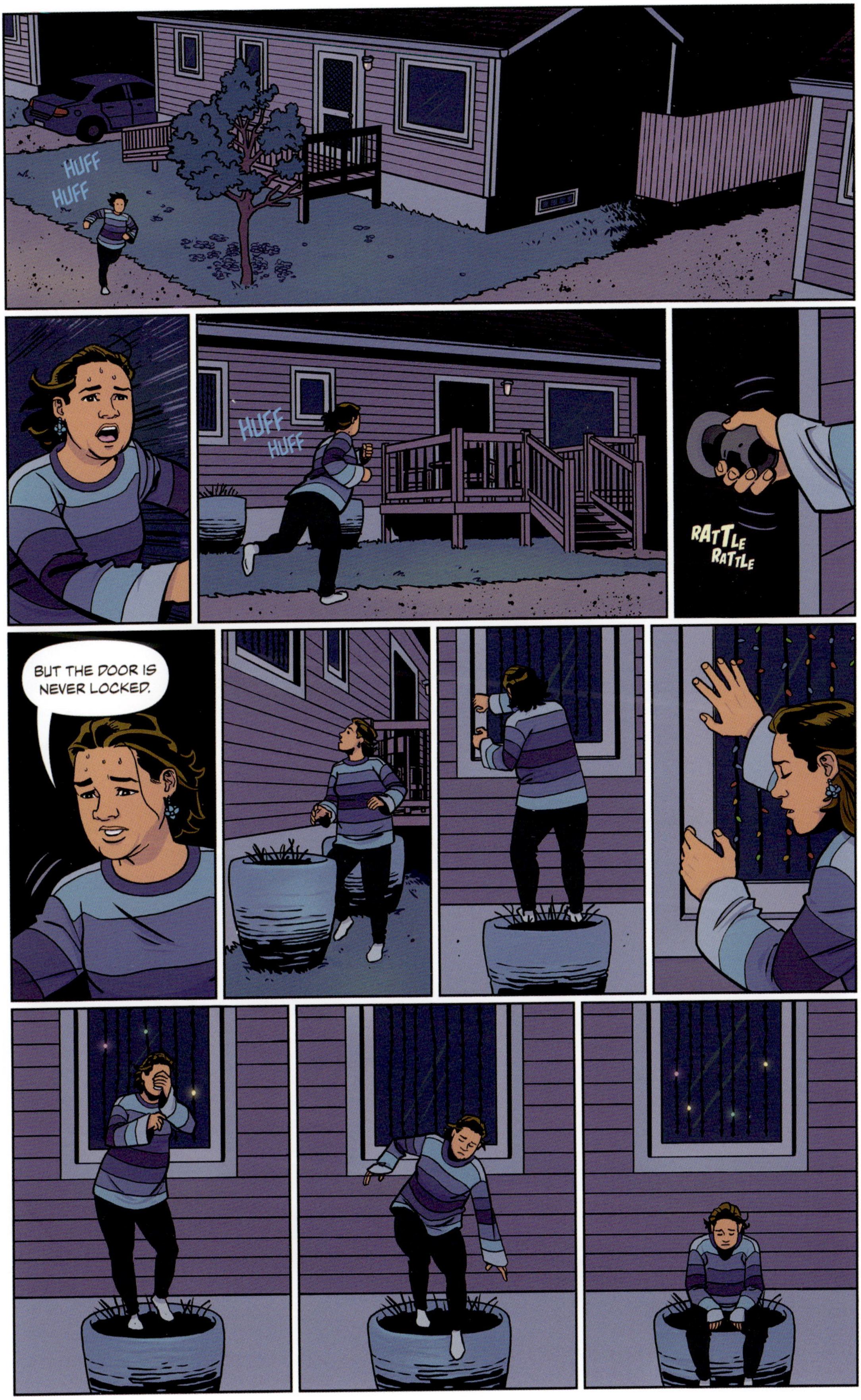
HUFF
HUFF
HUFF
HUFF
RATTLE
RATTLE
BUT THE DOOR IS NEVER LOCKED.

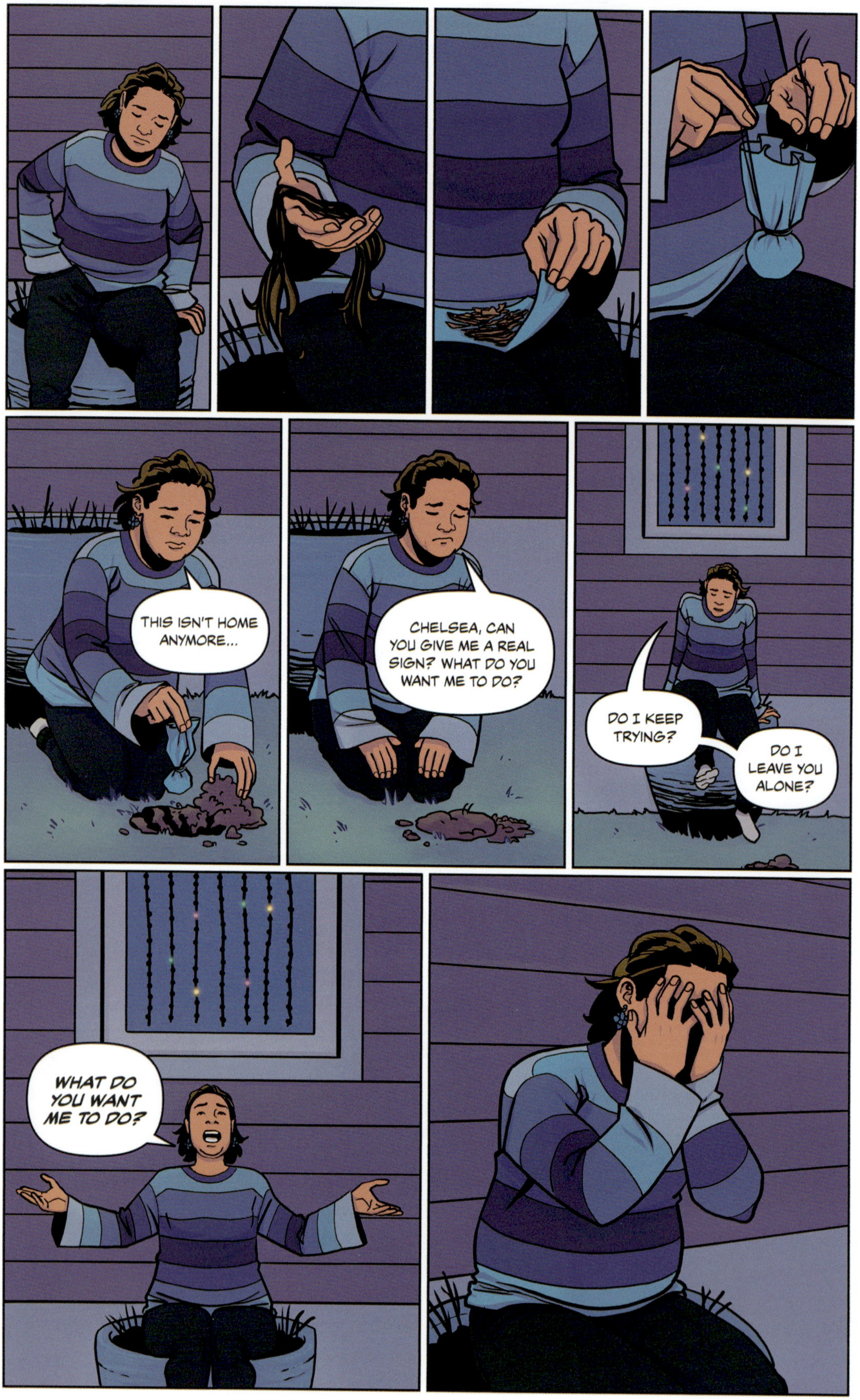
THIS ISN'T HOME ANYMORE...
CHELSEA, CAN YOU GIVE ME A REAL SIGN? WHAT DO YOU WANT ME TO DO?
DO I KEEP TRYING?
DO I LEAVE YOU ALONE?
WHAT DO YOU WANT ME TO DO?

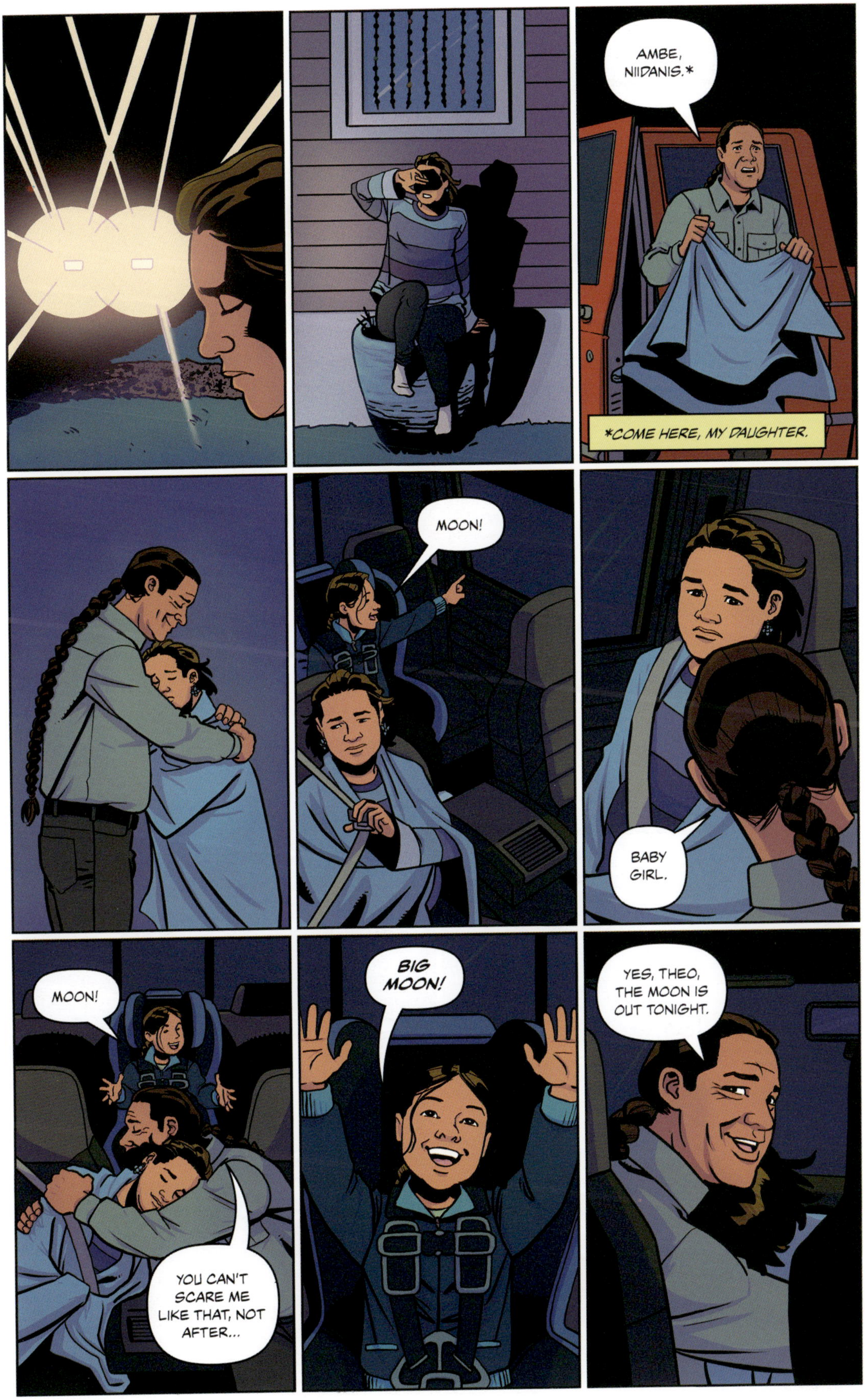
AMBE, NIIDANIS.*
*COME HERE, MY DAUGHTER.
MOON!
BABY GIRL.
MOON!
YOU CAN'T SCARE ME LIKE THAT, NOT AFTER...
BIG MOON!
YES, THEO, THE MOON IS OUT TONIGHT.

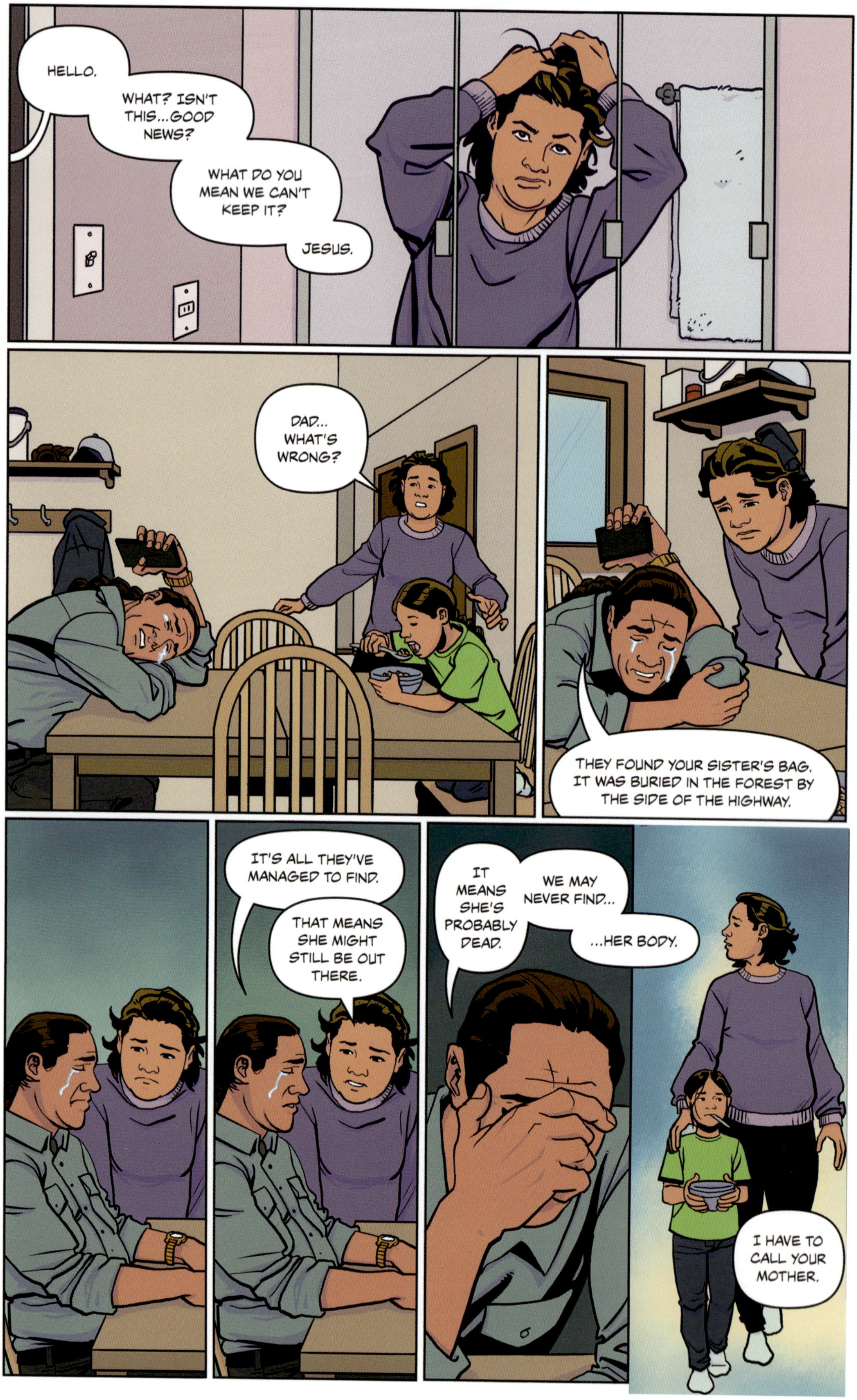
HELLO.
WHAT? ISN'T THIS...GOOD NEWS?
WHAT DO YOU MEAN WE CAN'T KEEP IT?
JESUS.
DAD... WHAT'S WRONG?
THEY FOUND YOUR SISTER'S BAG. IT WAS BURIED IN THE FOREST BY THE SIDE OF THE HIGHWAY.
IT'S ALL THEY'VE MANAGED TO FIND.
THAT MEANS SHE MIGHT STILL BE OUT THERE.
IT MEANS SHE'S PROBABLY DEAD.
WE MAY NEVER FIND...
...HER BODY.
I HAVE TO CALL YOUR MOTHER.

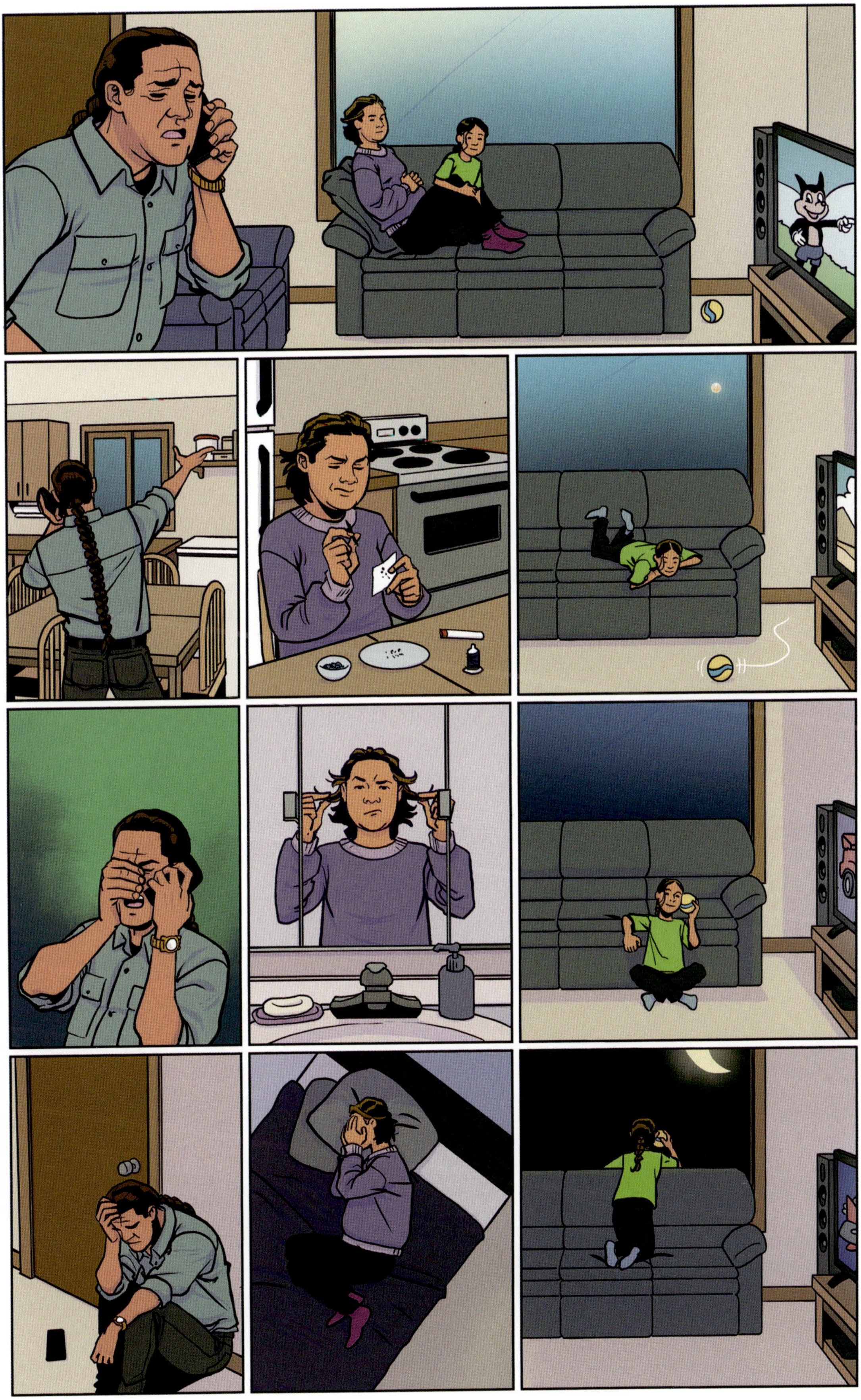

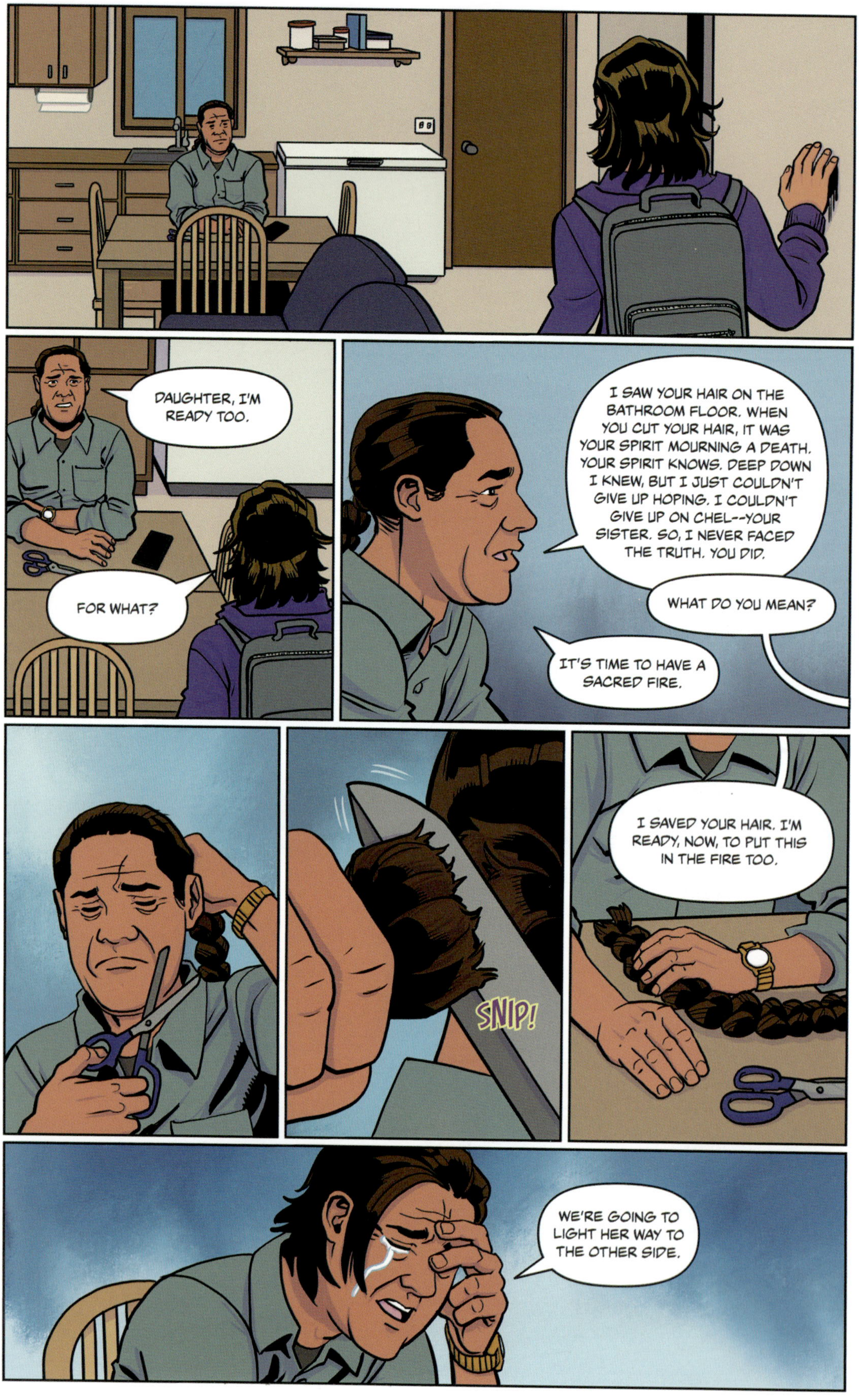
DAUGHTER, I'M READY TOO.
FOR WHAT?
I SAW YOUR HAIR ON THE BATHROOM FLOOR. WHEN YOU CUT YOUR HAIR, IT WAS YOUR SPIRIT MOURNING A DEATH. YOUR SPIRIT KNOWS. DEEP DOWN I KNEW, BUT I JUST COULDN'T GIVE UP HOPING. I COULDN'T GIVE UP ON CHEL--YOUR SISTER. SO, I NEVER FACED THE TRUTH. YOU DID.
WHAT DO YOU MEAN?
IT'S TIME TO HAVE A SACRED FIRE.
SNIP!
I SAVED YOUR HAIR. I'M READY, NOW, TO PUT THIS IN THE FIRE TOO.
WE'RE GOING TO LIGHT HER WAY TO THE OTHER SIDE.

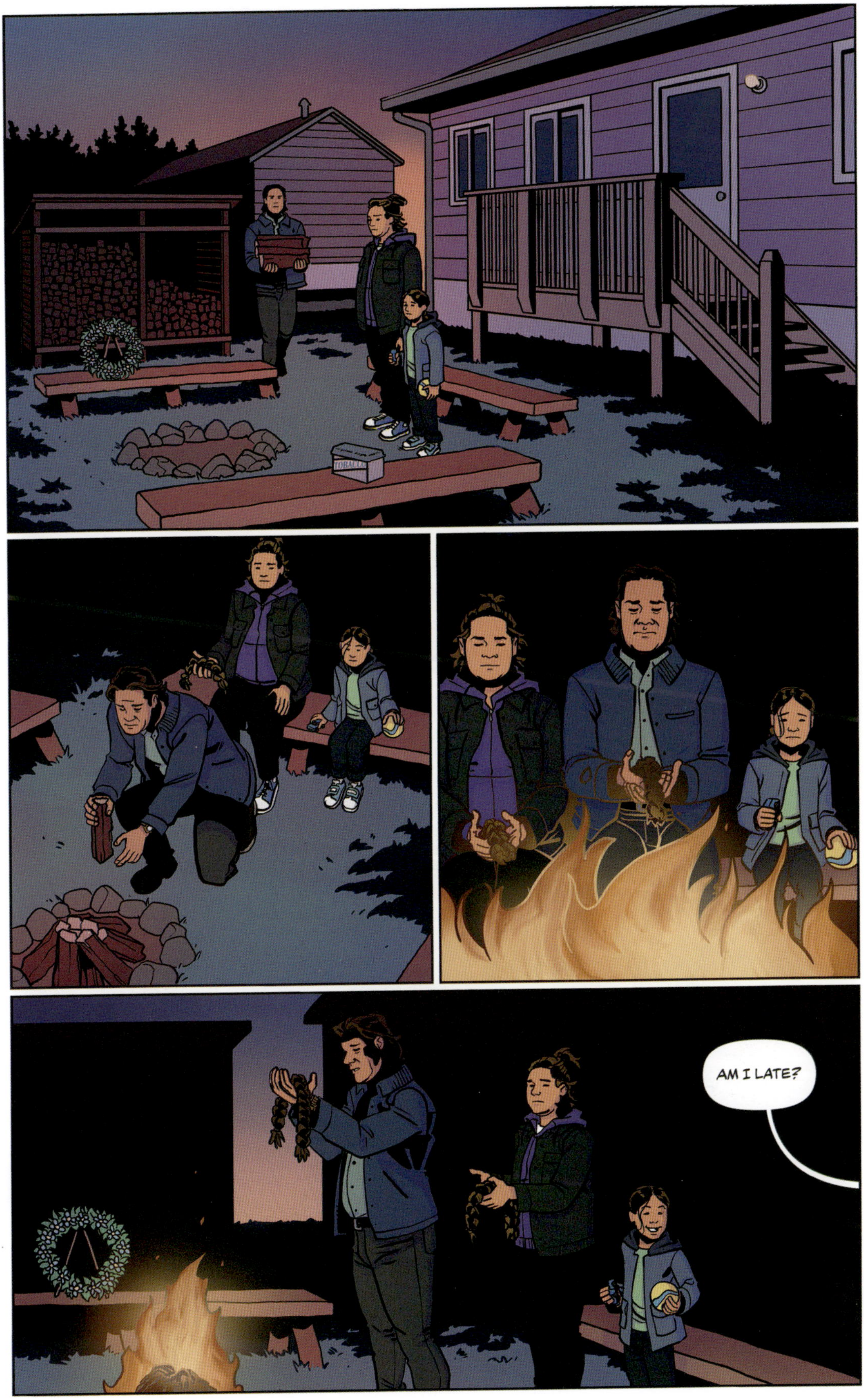
AM I LATE?

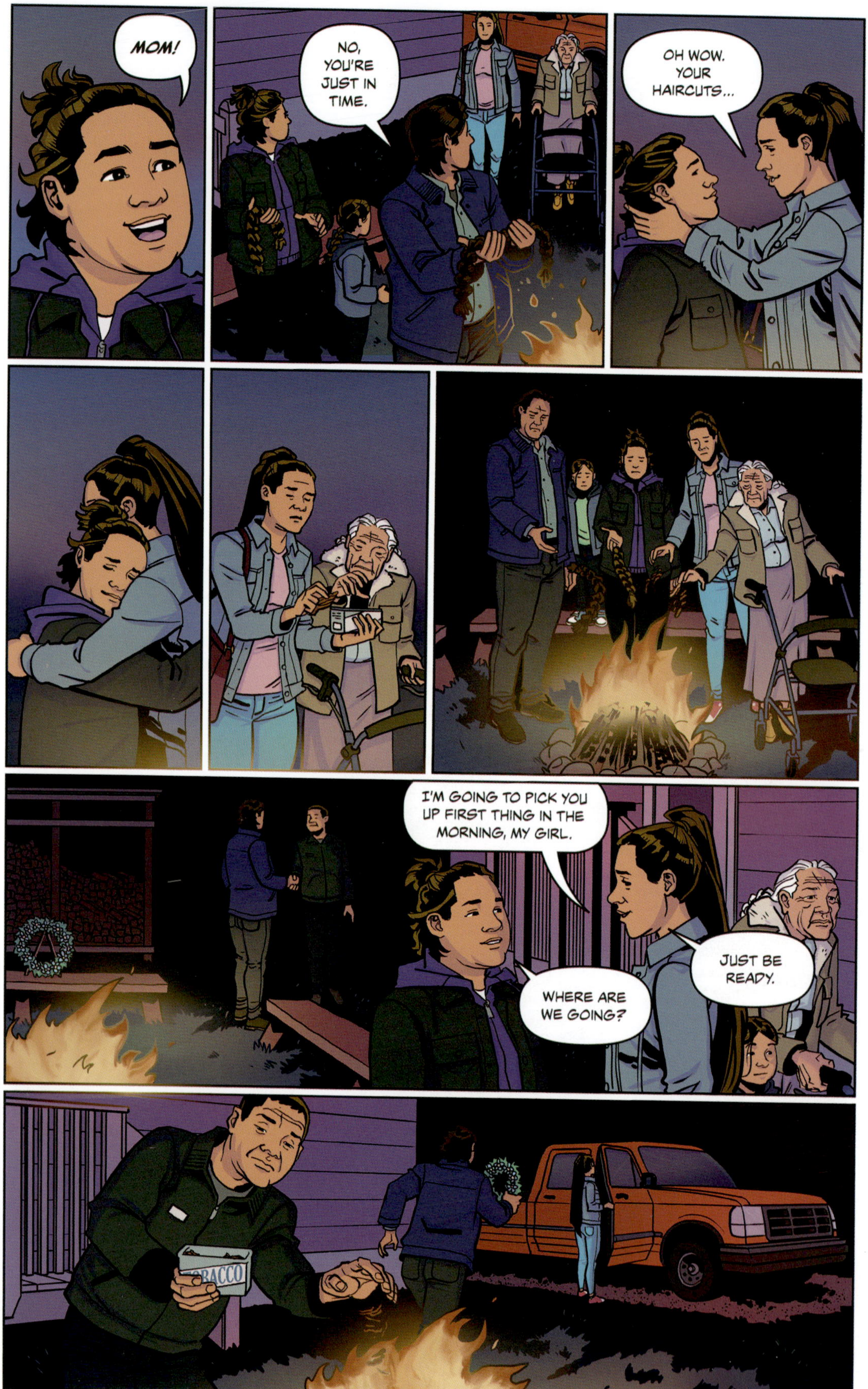
MOM!
NO, YOU'RE JUST IN TIME.
OH WOW. YOUR HAIRCUTS...
I'M GOING TO PICK YOU UP FIRST THING IN THE MORNING, MY GIRL.
WHERE ARE WE GOING?
JUST BE READY.
TOBACCO

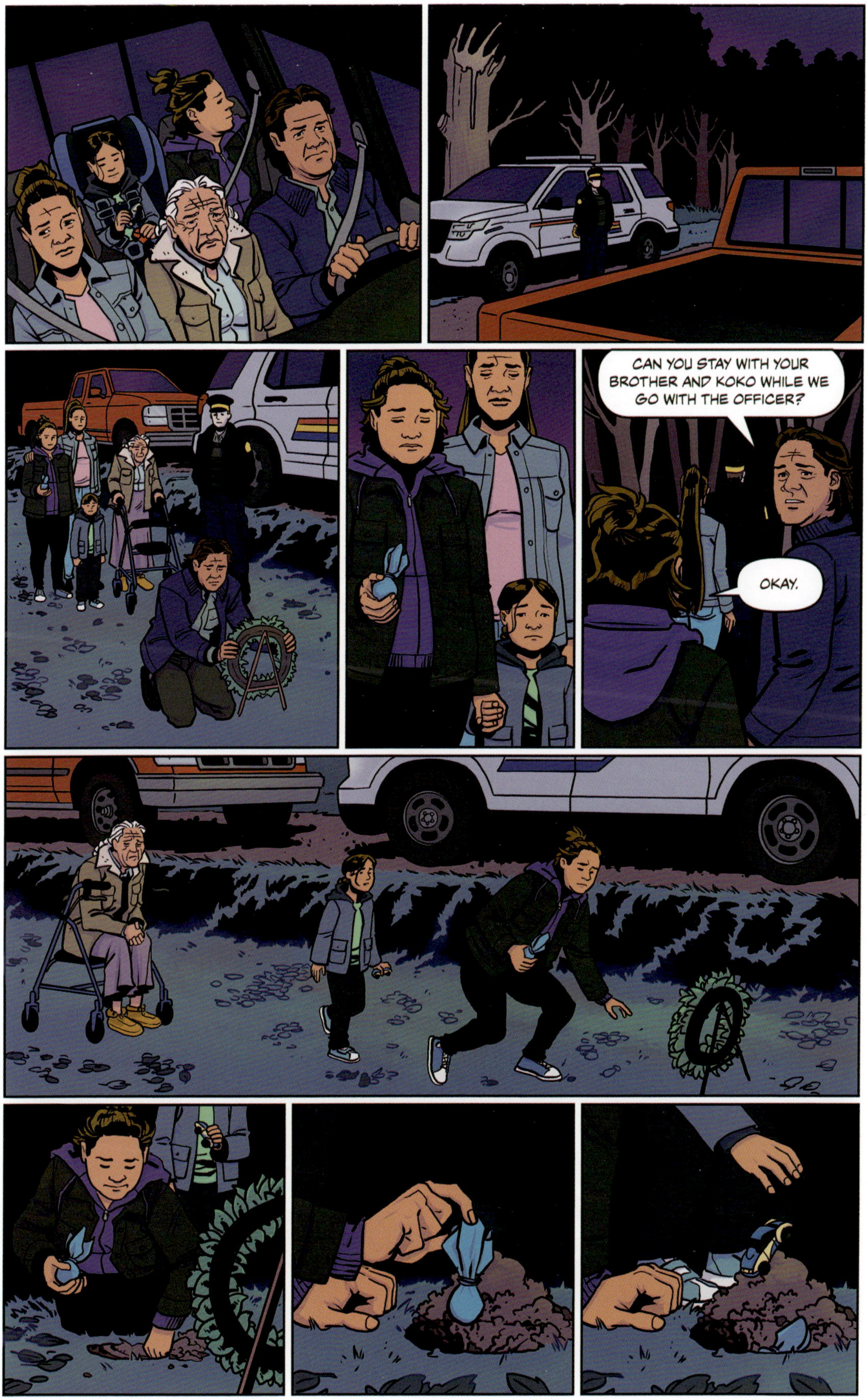
CAN YOU STAY WITH YOUR BROTHER AND KOKO WHILE WE GO WITH THE OFFICER?
OKAY.

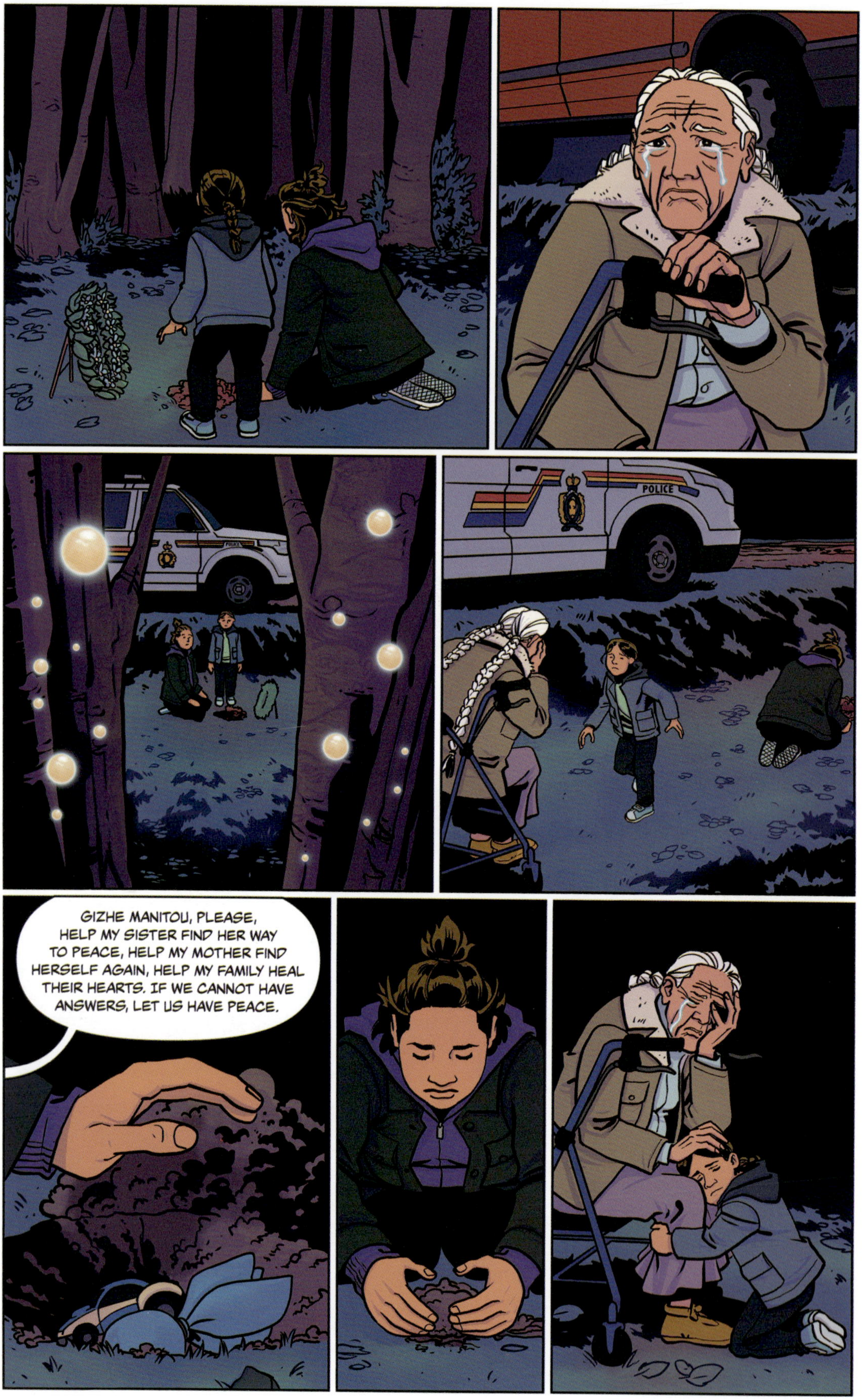
GIZHE MANITOU, PLEASE, HELP MY SISTER FIND HER WAY TO PEACE, HELP MY MOTHER FIND HERSELF AGAIN, HELP MY FAMILY HEAL THEIR HEARTS. IF WE CANNOT HAVE ANSWERS, LET US HAVE PEACE.

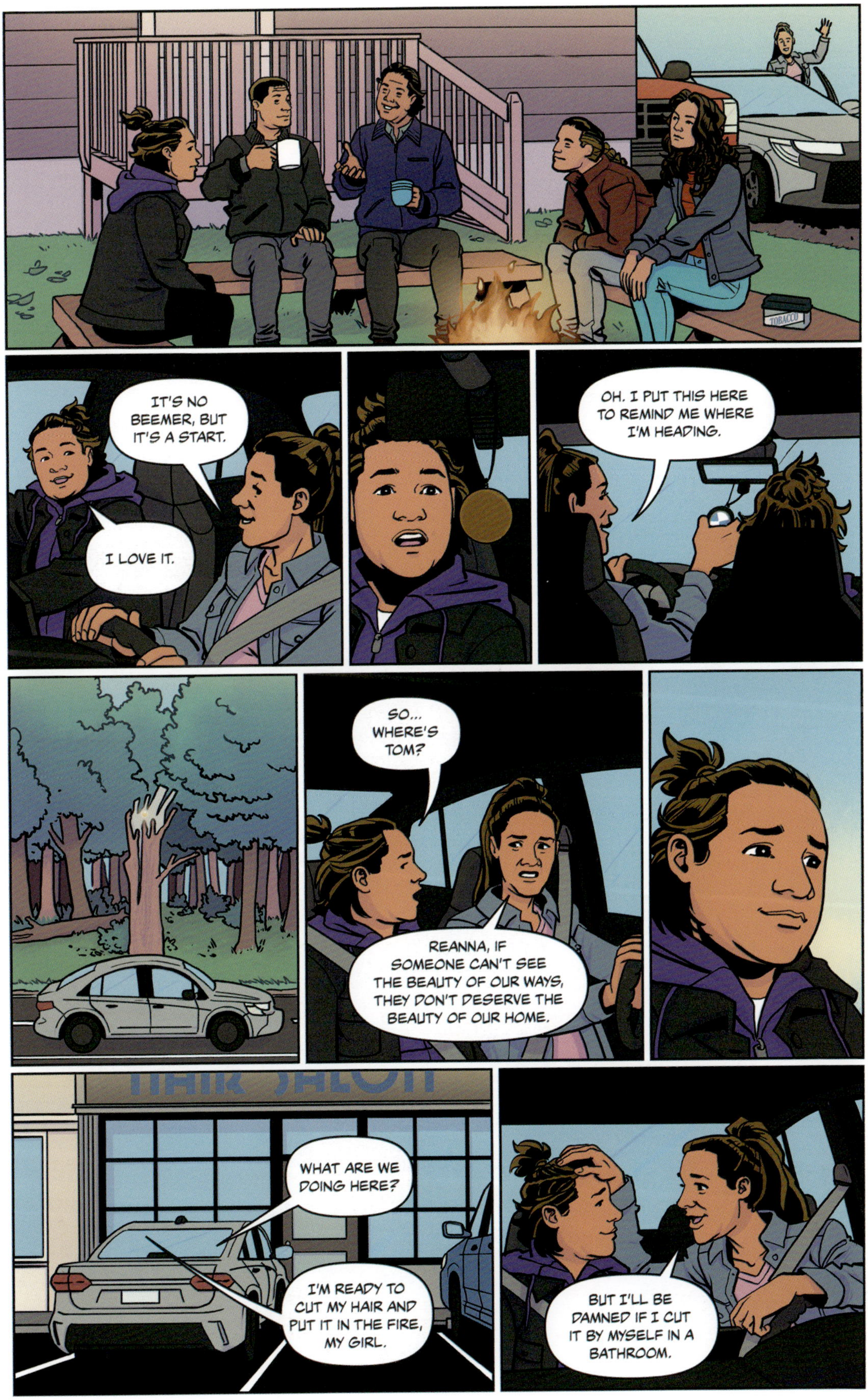
TOBACCO
IT'S NO BEEMER, BUT IT'S A START.
I LOVE IT.
OH. I PUT THIS HERE TO REMIND ME WHERE I'M HEADING.
SO... WHERE'S TOM?
REANNA, IF SOMEONE CAN'T SEE THE BEAUTY OF OUR WAYS, THEY DON'T DESERVE THE BEAUTY OF OUR HOME.
WHAT ARE WE DOING HERE?
I'M READY TO CUT MY HAIR AND PUT IT IN THE FIRE, MY GIRL.
BUT I'LL BE DAMNED IF I CUT IT BY MYSELF IN A BATHROOM.

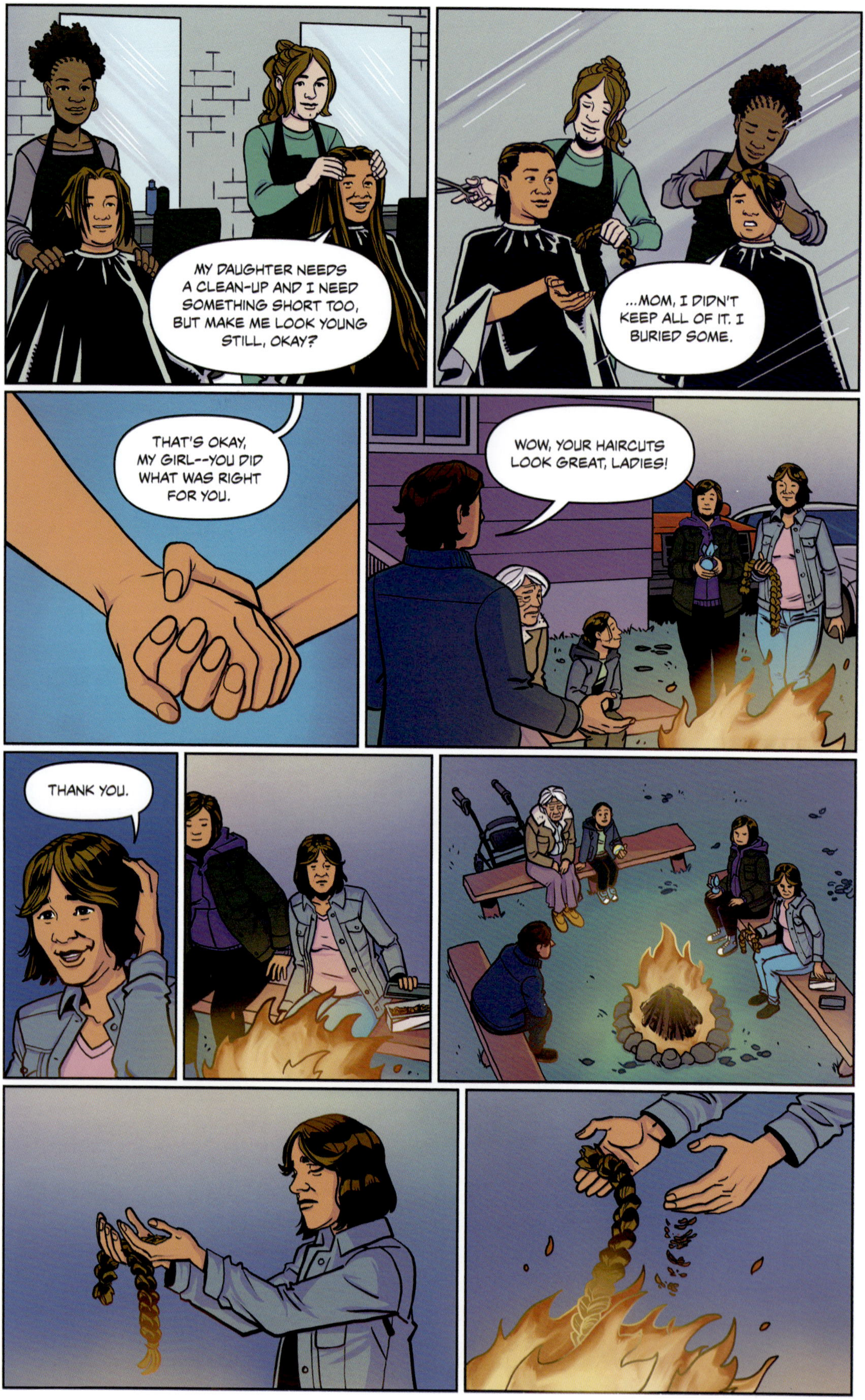
MY DAUGHTER NEEDS A CLEAN-UP AND I NEED SOMETHING SHORT TOO, BUT MAKE ME LOOK YOUNG STILL, OKAY?
...MOM, I DIDN'T KEEP ALL OF IT. I BURIED SOME.
THAT'S OKAY, MY GIRL--YOU DID WHAT WAS RIGHT FOR YOU.
WOW, YOUR HAIRCUTS LOOK GREAT, LADIES!
THANK YOU.

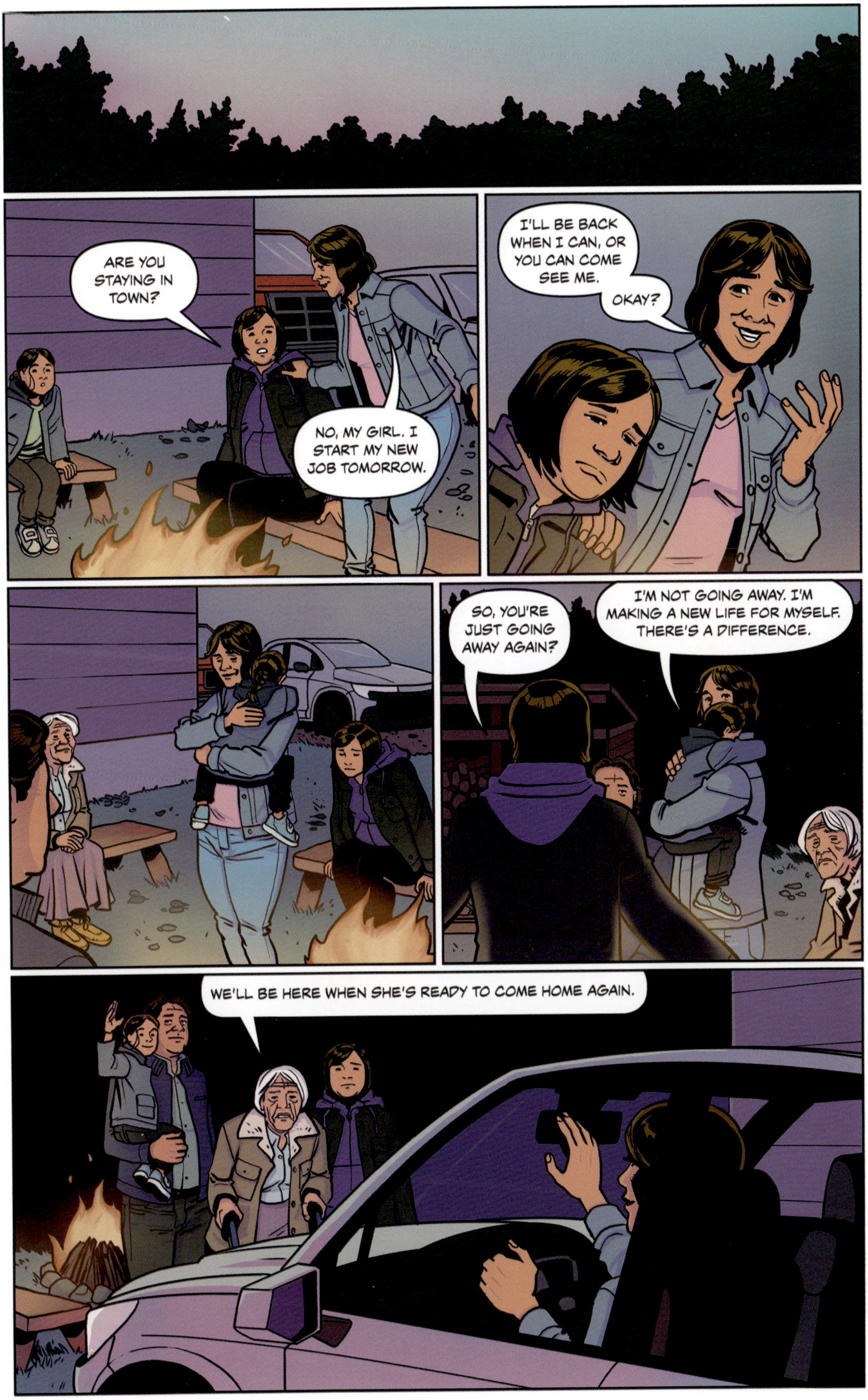
ARE YOU STAYING IN TOWN?
NO, MY GIRL. I START MY NEW JOB TOMORROW.
I'LL BE BACK WHEN I CAN, OR YOU CAN COME SEE ME.
OKAY?
SO, YOU'RE JUST GOING AWAY AGAIN?
I'M NOT GOING AWAY. I'M MAKING A NEW LIFE FOR MYSELF. THERE'S A DIFFERENCE.
WE'LL BE HERE WHEN SHE'S READY TO COME HOME AGAIN.

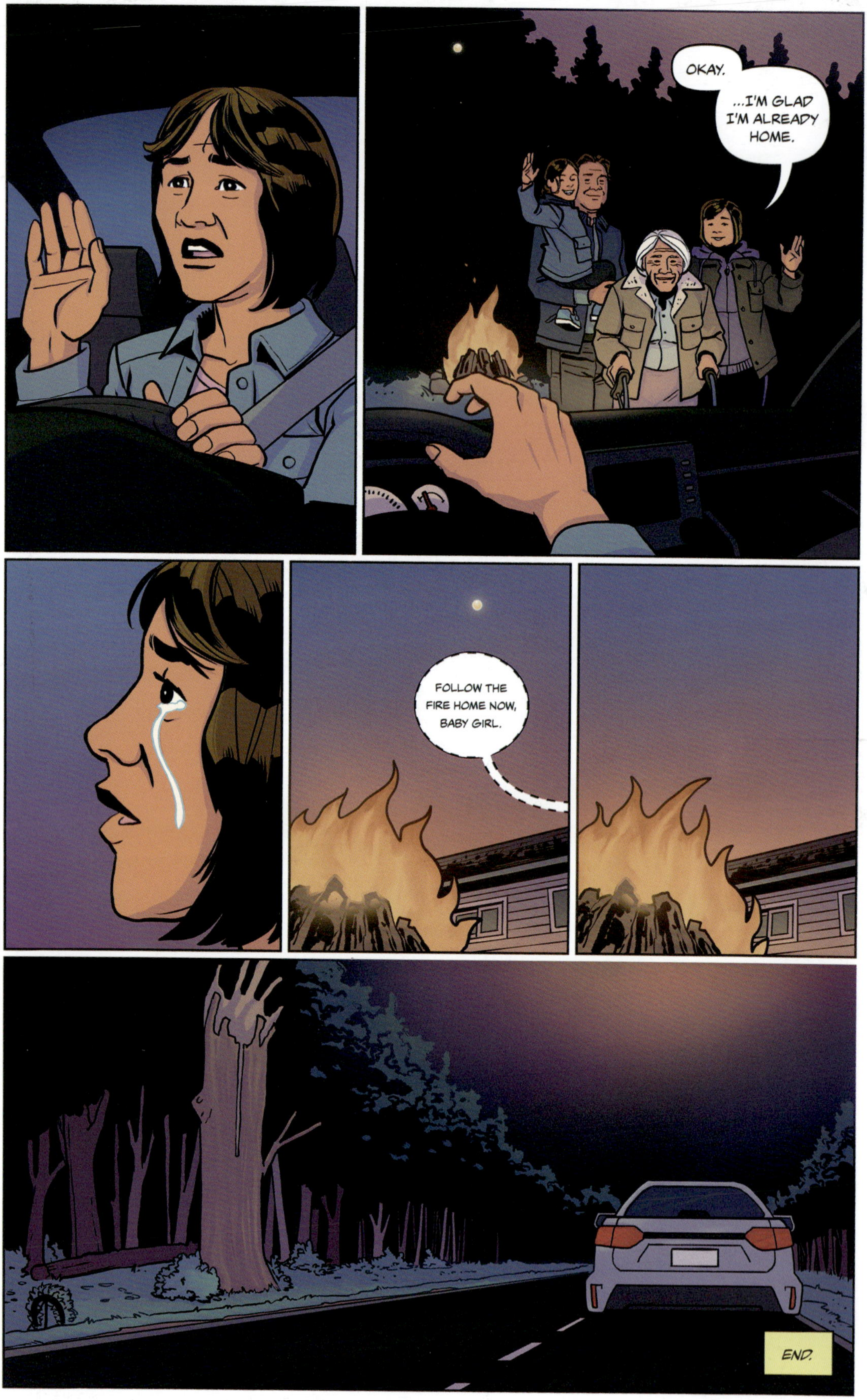
OKAY.
...I'M GLAD I'M ALREADY HOME.
FOLLOW THE FIRE HOME NOW, BABY GIRL.
END.

Little Moons is a complex personal story, so I wanted to share the ideas behind this book. The mourning traditions shown in this story represent my teachings, which are rooted in my own Ojibwe heritage. Although they are shared among various First Nations cultures, they do not encompass the entirety of First Nations or Ojibwe teachings across the country. I recognize the importance of honouring and respecting the diverse cultural teachings and traditional knowledges held by each community. It is vital that we honour and respect these differences as relatives on Turtle Island.

My experience with a loved one who went missing and was later found dead showed me a different kind of grief. I couldn't let go or grieve properly because so much was left unanswered. Nothing felt right, and justice never came. Grief is messy and complex; it's love with nowhere to go. Some people bury themselves in work or children, while others turn to unhealthy vices. While some readers may not relate to Andrea's character, I aimed to show a grieving mother. Although she's flawed, I hope readers empathize with her.

Chelsea's unresolved ending may also be hard to accept. While stories usually have neat endings, that's not the reality for many Indigenous women, girls, and Two-Spirit people. When a loved one goes missing, some families never get answers or closure, which I felt was important to show in *Little Moons*.

Beading is one way to express cultural teachings, make connections, and pass down traditions, skills, and values. Beadwork is a gift that says, "I am loved, important, and valued." Reanna beads to reconnect with her mother, but for Andrea, beading is a painful reminder that Chelsea is gone. In *Little Moons*, beading also represents Anthony's attempt to reconnect with Reanna.

Unlike the rest of the family, Theo can see Chelsea's spirit. My son, River, who inspired Theo's character, often saw spirits. When my childhood friend passed away, my son talked about seeing Aunty in his room. He said she came to him "like little moons." I've had inexplicable experiences throughout my life, so when my son did too, I knew I had to write *Little Moons*, if only to find a semblance of closure.

—*Jen Storm*

© 2024 Jen Storm (text)
© 2024 Ryan Howe (line art)

Excerpts from this publication may be reproduced with the prior written permission of Portage & Main Press Limited or under a licence from the Canadian Copyright Licensing Agency, Access Copyright.

All rights are reserved. This publication may not, in whole or in part, be reproduced, stored in a retrieval system, transmitted in any form or by any means—electronic, mechanical, photocopying, recording, or otherwise—or used to train any artificial intelligence device or software or otherwise incorporated or inputted in any artificial intelligence device or software.

HighWater Press gratefully acknowledges the financial support of the Government of Canada and Canada Council for the Arts as well as the Province of Manitoba through the Department of Sport, Culture, Heritage and Tourism and the Manitoba Book Publishing Tax Credit for our publishing activities.

HighWater Press is an imprint of Portage & Main Press
Printed and bound in Canada by Friesens
Design by Jennifer Lum
Cover art by Ryan Howe (line art) and Jason Lapidus (colours)
Colours by Alice RL
Lettering by Nickolej Villiger

Dedicated in loving memory to Ashten Eve Dawn Cook. —JEN STORM

For my incredibly patient family. —RYAN HOWE

Dedicated to my parents. —ALICE RL

For Indigenous families who have lost a loved one. —NICKOLEJ VILLIGER

Special thanks to Carl Stone for his cultural review of this work.

With thanks to the graphic arts student focus group from the Met Centre for Arts & Technology, Seven Oaks Met School, and Maples Met School (Winnipeg, MB) for their thoughtful feedback on the cover of this book.

Library and Archives Canada Cataloguing in Publication
Title: Little moons / [written by] Jen Storm ; [art by] Ryan Howe ;
[colours by] Alice RL ; [lettering by] Nickolej Villiger.
Names: Storm, Jen, 1986- author. | Howe, Ryan, artist. | RL, Alice, colorist. | Villiger, Nickolej, letterer.
Identifiers: Canadiana (print) 20240333209 | Canadiana (ebook) 20240333217
ISBN 9781774921074 (softcover) | ISBN 9781774921081 (EPUB) | ISBN 9781774921098 (PDF)
Subjects: LCGFT: Graphic novels. Classification: LCC PN6733.S765 L58 2024 | DDC j741.5/971—dc23

27 26 25 24   1 2 3 4 5

This book was printed in North America by Friesens, the first FSC-certified printing company in Canada. With plants powered by hydroelectric and wind farms, the company is 100% employee-owned and is committed to minimizing its ecological footprint. It is printed on FSC-certified paper using vegetable-based inks and alcohol-free blanket wash.

www.highwaterpress.com
Winnipeg, Manitoba
Treaty 1 Territory and homeland of the Métis Nation